His proposal was cold and dispassionate

She wasn't sure whether to laugh, cry, or scream abuse at him. He was joking, of course. He couldn't possibly be asking her to become his wife—could he?

But there was no sign of laughter on those rigidly handsome features, only a quiet brooding look.

"I'm told a proposal of marriage is normally preceded by a declaration of love," Liz informed him derisively.

"I haven't any love to offer you, but I do need a wife."

"You're saying you need a woman in your bed," she said bluntly.

"You'll never want for anything," he answered, moving closer.

"I want what you obviously can't give me," Liz replied with the direct honesty so true to her nature. "I want your love, Grant."

YVONNE WHITTAL
is also the author of these
Harlequin Romances

and these
Harlequin Presents

Many of these books are available at your local bookseller.

For a free catalog listing all titles currently available,
send your name and address to:

HARLEQUIN READER SERVICE
1440 South Priest Drive, Tempe, AZ 85281
Canadian address: Stratford, Ontario N5A 6W2

House of Mirrors

Yvonne Whittal

Harlequin Books

TORONTO • NEW YORK • LOS ANGELES • LONDON
AMSTERDAM • PARIS • SYDNEY • HAMBURG
STOCKHOLM • ATHENS • TOKYO • MILAN

Original hardcover edition published in 1982
by Mills & Boon Limited

ISBN 0-373-02538-6

Harlequin Romance first edition March 1983

CHAPTER ONE

THE early morning sunlight filtered into the bedroom through the lacy curtains at the window, and cast weird patterns on the bare wooden floor which had recently been stripped of its carpet. The smooth top of the chest of drawers was cluttered with an odd assortment of possessions ranging from a pile of much handled books, down to a porcelain eggcup in the shape of a chirpy, newly-hatched chick. The dressing-table top was in equal disarray, and a leather armchair provided a cushioned recess for a disorderly pile of records, a portable typewriter, a stack of neatly bound files, and several family photograph albums.

Birds fluttered in the trees outside the window, and some distance from the farm house a dog barked furiously, but Liz Holden was oddly reluctant to meet the challenge of this new day. She slid farther beneath the sheets, and buried her face in the pillow with a groan on her lips. She had worked until late the previous evening, sorting through possessions which had been gathered over a lifetime, discarding the useless, packing the necessary, and setting aside those which could possibly be added to the list for the public auctioneer. It was an unpleasant task, but one which circumstances had forced her to take upon herself. With Pamela in Canada, and Stacy in the final stages of her first pregnancy, Liz had had no option but to cope with the heartrending task of vacating the home she had known since childhood.

The telephone rang shrilly in the hall, shattering the tranquil silence in the large house, and Liz muttered a few uncomplimentary phrases as she scrambled out of bed and thrust her arms into the sleeves of an old cotton housecoat.

'I'm coming, I'm coming,' she grumbled irritably, not bothering to put anything on her feet as she rushed from her room. In the hall she accidentally kicked her foot against a wooden crate which stood in her way and, cursing loudly, she leaned over it and lifted the receiver off the hook. 'Yes, who is it?' she snapped into the mouthpiece, at the same time lifting her foot to nurse her injured toe with gentle fingers.

'You're in a foul mood on this bright sunny morning, I must say,' Stacy's disgustingly cheerful voice piped over the telephone.

'I was still in bed,' Liz informed her in a less aggressive tone.

'Good heavens! At eight-thirty in the morning?' Stacy exclaimed in mock horror. 'I've been up simply ages.'

'Well, good for you, but I only got to bed at two.'

'It must have been some party!'

Surrounded by the evidence of her backbreaking efforts the day before, Liz said cuttingly, 'That's not funny.'

'Sorry.' Stacy sobered at once. 'Don't lose your sense of humour, Liz.'

Liz lowered her foot gingerly to the floor and sighed inwardly. 'I'm trying not to.'

'Look, darling, what I'm actually phoning about is to tell you that Angus and I had a long chat last night, and we would be simply delighted if you would move in with us until you've decided what you're going to do.'

'That's very kind of you both, but——'

'No "buts", Liz,' Stacy interrupted in her warm, musical voice. 'Angus said I was to insist if you decided to act stubborn, and I'm insisting. Heaven knows there's plenty of room here, and I could certainly do with a few inspired ideas for the nursery.'

Liz smiled wryly to herself. 'You mean it's my inspired ideas and not my charming company which you desire so much?'

'Good, you're beginning to sound more like your usual self,' Stacy laughed. 'May I tell Angus that you've agreed to move in with us?'

'You may,' Liz's smile deepened. 'And thank you, Stacy.'

'I have a bit of gossip I'd like to pass on to you,' Stacy continued confidentially. 'Grant Battersby is back at High Ridges, and from what I've heard he's aiming to stay for quite some time.'

Feelings, suppressed and locked away for so many years, leapt to the fore and bundled Liz's insides into a tight knot. 'Where did you hear that?'

'Grant's farm manager, Sam Muller, brought one of the trucks in for a service yesterday, and he naturally told Angus.'

'I see.'

'Oh, well, I must hurry or I might be late for my appointment at the hairdresser.'

Stacy hung up, and Liz went slowly back to her room where she sat curled up on her bed, her arms hugging her knees up under her chin as the years rolled away, and memories suffused her mind.

There were memories of a childhood without the mother who had died when Liz was four, but her father had seen to it that she enjoyed happy, carefree years of much laughter, and very few tears. Grant Battersby had featured prominently through all those years of growing up; a tall, dark, handsome fourth to the trio of Holden girls, but it had been Pamela, the eldest and by far the prettiest, who had been the main attraction.

The period Liz could remember most vividly was the year she had turned sixteen. She had hero-worshipped Grant as a child, but suddenly, at sixteen, she developed a king-size crush on him which had been so intense at the time that her bones had melted whenever he had appeared—and, with Riverside adjoining High Ridges, that had been quite often. Grant had, of course, been quite oblivious of these shattering emotions he had so inadvertently aroused in Liz Holden, the cheeky tomboy with the corn-coloured pigtails, and she would have died rather than have him discover how she had felt about him.

At that time Grant had been a man of twenty-eight, and he was literally carving a name for himself in the field of surgery, but he was also one of the many men Pamela had amused herself with. Pamela had then been a fair strikingly beautiful twenty-four, and 'more than ready for marriage', their father had always grumbled, but Pamela had shied away from the thought of a husband and a family as if it were the plague. Stacy, two years younger than Pamela, had been equally fair, but she had been pretty rather than beautiful, and her quiet, sensible nature had ensnared the attentions of Angus MacLeod, a fiery Scot who had emigrated to South Africa as a child, and had worked himself up into the position where he was the owner of a thriving service station in Pietersburg.

Liz had always been an impossible child, but at sixteen she had been quite a terror. Her sharp, often mocking tongue had voiced her thoughts regardless of the consequences, and it had often landed her in dire straits with the family. Her most closely guarded secret had been her feelings for Grant; that had been something she had never spoken about, and wild horses would not have dragged this information from her.

Christmas that year was one Liz had never forgotten. It had been, as always, a scorchingly hot summer in the northern Transvaal, and the festivities had been celebrated in the sweltering heat with frequent trips to the river in attempts to revive themselves in the cool, flowing waters. There had been quite a crowd of young people at Riverside that day, and Myra Cavendish had been among them. No one quite knew who had invited Myra, but they had all known that she had had her sights set on Grant for quite some time, and Grant fell that day for the seductive charm of that green-eyed beauty. He had fallen like a weighty sinker plummeting the depths of the river, and Liz had been sick at the thought of Myra's easy victory.

Nothing had been quite the same since. Myra departed for Johannesburg to continue with her modelling career, and Grant had followed her shortly afterwards.

During the six years following that Christmas Liz had seen Grant only once, and then very briefly. His parents had died tragically in a car accident, and he had arrived at High Ridges for the funeral, but he had left almost immediately afterwards, and a month later Sam Muller and his family had been installed in the homestead as manager. A small cottage had been erected close to the banks of the river where Grant could stay whenever he wished to visit the large cattle estate, but the cottage had remained empty except for the furnishings. Stacy married Angus two years after the untimely death of Grant's parents, and she had set up a home in Pietersburg. A few months later Pamela left for Canada to pursue a career as a beauticianal adviser. Liz went off to university to study for her B.A. in literature, but instead of accepting a teaching post she returned home to her father and indulged in her lifetime dream of writing stories for children. Her father had been horrified at the time, but her books had sold, and now, six months after his death, she was firmly established in her literary career.

Liz had always dreaded receiving the news that Grant Battersby had married Myra Cavendish, but it had never materialised over the years. Their affair had simply continued without the restrictions of marriage ... until four months ago. The news of their engagement, barely two months after her father's sudden death, had left Liz shattered, but she had rallied with characteristic swiftness. That was that, she had told herself, but there were more shocks in store for her. A month after his engagement to Myra was announced Grant was involved in an accident which left him with a leg broken in several places, cracked ribs, and a severely damaged hand. Myra, typically, deserted him when he must have needed her most, and now, three months after rolling his car down an embankment, Liz was told that Grant had returned to High Ridges. His future as a surgeon was doubtful, or so it had been rumoured, and the woman he had hoped to marry had taken herself off to some European country with a man almost twice her age.

'Poor Grant,' Liz thought, her compassionate heart aching for him as she slid off the bed and went into the bathroom to run her bath water. Later in the morning, perhaps, she would pay him a neighbourly visit.

It was not until that afternoon, however, that Liz had the opportunity to go out to High Ridges, and she was uncommonly nervous when she cycled along the much-trodden path towards the gate which divided the two properties. During happier times this particular gate had been used often by Grant and the Holden girls, but now it was chained and padlocked in a manner which said clearly, 'Keep out!'

Liz propped her bicycle up against a tree, and with her left foot firmly planted in the fencing wire attached to the steel gate, she pulled herself up and swung her right leg over the top. Her left leg followed smartly, but a brief second before she would have leapt to the ground she caught sight of a movement beside the old mopani tree which stood barely ten paces away.

It was Grant! She would have known him anywhere, she thought, and her heart knocked against her ribs in that old familar way. He was leaning heavily on a stick, his wide shoulders hunched, and his dark head bent. He looked weary, and he was quite a considerable distance from the cottage he was occupying for the first time in so many years.

So engrossed was he in his thoughts that he had obviously not heard her arrive and, maintaining her perch on the gate, she said in her warm, faintly husky voice, 'Welcome home, Grant.'

He turned at once, his head lifting, and the smile froze on her lips when she found herself looking into those steel-grey eyes. There was a hostility there which she did not understand, but she did not linger on the reason for it as she took this opportunity to study him more closely. There were premature silver wings in the dark hair against his temples, and his skin appeared to be stretched too tightly across his cheek-bones and down to his square jaw. He looked almost ten years older than his thirty-four years, and the perfectly chiselled, often sensuous mouth, was drawn into a thin, hard line of displeasure.

Grant, in turn, was studying her, taking in her slim, boyish figure in faded blue jeans and white cotton shirt, but there was nothing boyish about the small, firm breasts straining against the confining material, nor the corn-coloured hair which had been pulled back from her face and held together in the nape of her neck with a narrow yellow ribbon.

'What do you want?' he demanded, an unfamiliar harshness in his deep, well-modulated voice.

'A simple "hello" would do for a start.'

'Hello . . . and goodbye.'

His rudeness startled her, and her eyes, more gold than brown, clouded as she studied him intently for a moment before she said: 'You're not very sociable, are you?'

'Why don't you go home and play with your dolls?' he suggested with cold sarcasm, gesturing violently with his stick.

'I'm twenty-two, Grant.' The corners of her mouth quivered with the effort to hide her smile, but her eyes mocked him openly. 'Girls my age don't play with dolls any more.'

'No, they play with men, and the game is to see how many of them they can twist around their little fingers before they drop them flat.'

'I don't think I'd like to have a man wrapped around my little finger,' she replied gravely, but a spark of humour still lurked in her eyes. 'It would be rather uncomfortable—for the man, I mean.'

Not a flicker of a smile crossed his thin face, and neither did he remark upon her statement. He merely pointed once again with his stick and said testily, 'Must you perch so precariously on that gate?'

'I'll climb down if you promise not to strike me with that stick you're waving about so threateningly.'

'With the fence between us that's hardly likely to happen.'

If he had struck her physically she could not have been more surprised, and her hands tightened involuntarily on the gate. 'You're not inviting me on to Battersby property, then?'

'No, I'm not.'

This hostile, harsh man was not the Grant Battersby she had known all those years ago, but she simply could not, and would not believe that he had changed to such an extent. 'You weren't always this unfriendly. I can remember when——'

'That was a long time ago,' he interrupted in a cold, clipped voice.

'Before you made a fool of yourself over that Cavendish woman, yes,' she agreed sharply, but she could have bitten off her tongue the next instant when she saw his face become distorted with fury.

His eyes were like frozen chips of ice, and his voice had the biting chill of the Arctic in it when he said: 'Get off that gate, and if you know what's good for you, you'll stay off my property!'

He did not wait to see whether she obeyed him, but limped away, and Liz's eyes clouded with pain as she watched him for a few seconds, then she swung her legs over the gate and climbed down, to find that her legs were shaky as she walked to where she had left her bicycle.

Confused and bewildered, she cycled back the way she had come. Her friendly intentions had been misconstrued, and her advances had met with an open hostility which troubled her intensely. She had had no right, of course, to mock his feelings for Myra Cavendish, but then she had been severely provoked, and now Battersby property was forbidden to her.

When Stacy telephoned that evening she groaned loudly when Liz told her of her encounter with Grant that afternoon.

'When will you learn to hold your tongue, Liz,' Stacy rebuked her. 'You'll have to send him a written apology.'

'I'll do better than that. I'll pay him a formal visit tomorrow afternoon, and apologise personally.'

'Take care that you don't get a load of buckshot where it hurts most,' Stacy warned laughingly.

'It's worth the risk,' Liz informed her adamantly.

'I don't know why you're going to all this trouble. The man obviously wants to be left alone.'

'He needs help, Stacy.'

'Don't be ridiculous!' her sister exploded. 'Grant has always been totally self-sufficient, and if I were you I'd leave him alone to sort himself out all in his own good time.'

Stacy's advice was always sound, but on this occasion Liz ignored it, and the following afternoon she cycled down to the river. Grant's cottage was not too far from the fence which formed a boundary between the two farms and, propping her bicycle up against a thorn tree, she climbed over the barbed wire fence and walked along the river's edge.

It was a hot February afternoon and, flushed and perspiring from her ride, she dipped her handkerchief in the water and wiped her face. It left her feeling cool and refreshed, but when she straightened from her task she caught sight of a movement to her right.

'Grant,' his name slipped nervously from her lips when she saw him limping slowly towards her, but she remained where she was, her glance taking in his tall, muscled frame in beige denims, and green open-necked shirt. He had lost a considerable amount of weight, but he had lost none of that inner vitality she remembered so well.

'I thought I told you——'

'I've come to apologise,' she interrupted him hastily. 'I should have had my tongue clipped years ago.' She pushed her damp handkerchief into the pocket of her jeans and tilted her head back to look a long way up into those grey eyes observing her so dispassionately. 'Am I forgiven?'

He did not reply at once, but she saw the tightening of the muscles along the side of his jaw before he said abruptly, 'Go home, Liz.'

'So you *do* remember my name,' she smiled up at him impishly, determined not to be discouraged by his hostile attitude. 'I was beginning to think you'd forgotten.'

'You haven't changed much,' he observed derisively. 'You were always an impossible child, and it's obvious that you've grown into an impossible young woman.'

Her smile deepened. 'Liz, the horror of the Holden family, that's me.'

'You remembered that?' he asked, his eyebrows raised in faint surprise.

'I've remembered everything you've ever said to me,' she replied, adding with blatant and disarming honesty, 'Didn't you know that I had a crush on you once? When I was sixteen, to be exact?'

Her confession had the desired effect. The coldness left his eyes, to be replaced by a gleam of sardonic amusement. 'You have, I hope, outgrown it?'

'Oh, yes,' she replied flippantly. 'As my Prince Charming you fell from grace when I caught you kissing my sister Pamela in the apple orchard behind the house.'

His mouth twitched, but his expression remained unaltered as he remarked cynically, 'You've found yourself a more worthy Prince Charming since, I'm sure.'

'I haven't exactly been looking for one,' she shrugged, looking away from him towards the river, but something in his silence made her glance back at him. His face had gone quite white, and she saw for the first time the livid little scars against the back of the hand which was massaging his right leg. 'Does it hurt very much?'

'Mind your own business!'

'Don't be so damn touchy!' she retaliated swiftly.

'I don't need and neither do I want your concern,' he virtually snarled at her.

'My concern was for myself,' she informed him in a voice which was devoid of sympathy. 'If you collapse at my feet I'm hardly in a position to carry you home, am I?'

'I must sit down,' he confessed at length.

'This is the best place, I think,' she said, pointing to a grassy patch beneath the shade of the willows, and it was with the greatest difficulty that she refrained from offering her assistance when he lowered himself awkwardly on to the grass.

Liz sat down a little distance from him, her anxious

eyes observing him unobtrusively when he popped a
tablet into his mouth and lay back with his arm raised
over his face. Was there any real truth in the rumour
that his career as a surgeon was at an end? Her eyes
sought his scarred hand, but when she recalled how he
had handled the walking stick the previous day she
could not quite believe that his hand had lost its flexibility to that extent, and even though she longed to
question him about it, she knew that she dared not.

'You're unusually quiet,' Grant finally broke the
silence between them, and her golden gaze locked with
his.

'I didn't imagine you were in the mood for making
conversation.'

'I'm not, as a matter of fact,' he said drily.

'Then we won't talk.'

She hugged her knees up beneath her chin, and
stared out across the river which paved its way so relentlessly through both High Ridges and Riverside. As
children they had bathed in it often, and the smooth
golden tan of her skin was evidence of the fact that Liz
still indulged in this pleasurable pastime.

She sat there for a long time, immersed in her
own thoughts, with only the birds in the trees for company, and the slow, even breathing of the man who lay
on the grass a little distance from her. He had fallen
asleep, quite probably as a result of the tablet he had
taken, but, whatever the cause, she had no desire to
wake him. In sleep he looked more like the Grant she
had known and loved as a young girl of sixteen, and if it
were not for the abundance of grey hair against his
temples, then she could almost make herself believe
that they had gone back in time to those happy, carefree days before Myra Cavendish had appeared on the

scene. Myra had whisked him out of their lives with her bewitching ways, and now, after six years, she had thrust him back, a mentally crushed and embittered man.

A lump rose in Liz's throat, but she swallowed it down forcibly and looked away from his sleeping form. The clouds were building up in the sky, and if she was not mistaken they would have rain before nightfall. They could do with a good rain to soak the parched, crusty earth, she thought, and she sighed audibly.

'Have I been asleep?' Grant's deep voice startled her into an awareness of his presence.

'You have,' she informed him abruptly and, glancing up at the sky, she added: 'I must go home.'

'I suppose your father must be wondering what's——'

'My father died six months ago,' she interrupted him in a brittle voice, getting to her feet and brushing the dry grass off the seat of her jeans.

'I didn't know. I'm sorry,' he muttered apologetically, levering himself up on to his feet.

'Riverside has been sold, but the new owners very kindly allowed me to stay on in the house until the end of this month. That means I have a little less than two weeks left to vacate the place, and I'm finding it rather an awesome task trying to decide what to keep, and what to put up for sale by public auction.'

Grant fumbled in his shirt pocket for his cigarettes and lit one. 'Where will you go?'

'I shall be staying with Stacy and Angus in Pietersburg for a while. They offered to have me until I decide what to do, and where to go.'

An awkward silence followed, then he glanced up at the sky and echoed her thoughts of a few moments ago. 'There's a storm brewing.'

'In more ways than one,' she thought wryly, listening to the labouring beat of her own heart, but aloud she said: 'You're welcome to drop in at Riverside while I'm still in residence.'

'Thank you.'

'But you won't, will you,' she said stiffly, sensing his rejection of her friendly invitation. 'You'd rather withdraw into yourself than seek out the company of an old friend.'

She bit down hard on her wayward tongue, but it was too late. Those words had been spoken, and there was no way she could retract them.

'You'd better go, Liz, or you might find yourself caught in the rain.'

His voice was polite, but acid, and her hands made a helpless gesture of apology before she turned from him and walked quickly to where she had left her bicycle. She climbed over the fence, aware of his eyes following every move she made, and a prickly sensation coursed its way up her spine as she pedalled away at a furious pace.

Liz was kept too busy during the next two weeks to give much thought to Grant, although there had been a few evenings when she had sat amidst the chaos of what had once been her home, and loneliness and misery had driven her to wonder whether he might not, perhaps, consider accepting her invitation. It had been wishful thinking, of course, and it had been just as well that he had stayed away, for Liz had rarely been in a fit state to entertain visitors after the hectic days of packing her belongings and arranging for the disposal of the furniture.

It rained again on the day of the auction, but the auctioneer seemed confident of drawing a large crowd, and he was right. The large, rambling house almost burst its seams, and moving from one room to the other with the breezy auctioneer was a near impossible task. Tired, and irritable in the extreme, Liz shouldered and elbowed her way out among the perspiring bodies into the fresh air on the wide stoop, and she considered herself lucky to escape only with a few bruises instead of several crushed toes.

Two interminable hours later it was all over, and the driveway was empty when Liz wandered back into the silent house. The auctioneer's stickers had been thumbed on to every conceivable piece of furniture, and muddy footprints intermingled on the wooden floorboards. This was her last night in her old home with these familiar objects around her. They would all be collected in the morning, and her meagre possessions would be transported to Stacy's house in Pietersburg.

Tears filled her eyes, but she dashed them away hastily. This was not the time for weeping. There was still too much to do, she scolded herself mentally, but a strong cup of tea would be a good idea to settle those nerves which quivered at the pit of her stomach. The kitchen was still blessedly untouched by the hordes who had roamed the house that morning, and Liz moved about automatically, making herself a cup of tea, and forcing herself to sit down quietly at the table while she drank it. There was still plenty to do, but it could wait a few minutes longer.

She slept fitfully that night, and was awake long before dawn. Liz had been up three hours when the first truck arrived shortly after seven to cart away some of the furniture, and it was midday before she herself drove away from Riverside. Her father's old station wagon was loaded, and she knew that she would have to make a return trip that afternoon to pick up the few items which had been left behind.

A half hour later she was parked in the driveway of Stacy's home, and Stacy's maid swiftly organised the young garden boy into helping with the unloading of Liz's belongings.

'Come in out of the heat,' said Stacy, slipping her arm through Liz's and taking her into the spacious house with its cool, modern furnishings. 'You look exhausted,' she observed, eyeing Liz critically with her brown, doe-like eyes.

Liz found herself studying her sister just as critically when they entered the living-room. 'I could almost say the same about you.'

Stacy lowered herself into a chair and rolled her eyes towards the ceiling. 'As Angus would say, the wee lad's becoming rather hefty.'

'You seem very sure it's going to be a boy,' Liz grinned, seating herself on a chair close to Stacy's, and realising for the first time how tired she actually was when it felt to her as if every muscle in her body was aching.

'Angus is positive it's going to be a boy, but I don't very much care what it is as long as it's strong, healthy, and arrives soon.'

'You haven't very much longer to wait.'

'Darling,' Stacy laughed ruefully, patting her well-rounded stomach, 'in my condition a week could feel like a year!' Their eyes met, and Stacy sobered instantly. 'I'm sorry you had to do it all on your own, Liz.'

'It couldn't be helped,' Liz brushed the matter aside abruptly.

The selling of Riverside was a subject neither of them enjoyed discussing, and after a strained little silence Stacy directed the conversation along a different channel. 'Have you seen anything of Grant lately?'

'Not since the day I called on him to apologise for my runaway tongue.' Liz fingered the pleats in her skirt and frowned. 'He's changed, Stacy.'

'In what way?'

'Well, apart from the fact that he looks a great deal older than he actually is, he—he's terribly embittered, and cynical somehow.'

'Wouldn't you be embittered and cynical if you were in his position?'

'I suppose so, but . . .' Liz thumped her clenched fist into the padded arm of the chair. 'Dammit, Stacy, it's not the end of the world, you know.'

'Tell that to *him*, little sister,' Stacy murmured drily.

'You know something,' Liz retorted. 'I might just do that.'

After a light lunch Liz drove out to Riverside to collect the things she had been forced to leave behind earlier, but before returning to Pietersburg she turned in at High Ridges and took the bumpy dual-strip track to Grant's cottage.

With whitewashed walls and tiled roof, it looked neat and compact where it nestled among the willow and acacia trees a little distance from the river. A sleek white Jaguar was parked in the car-port alongside the cottage, and Liz's heart was suddenly thumping hard and fast against her ribs when she climbed out of the station-wagon and approached the front door. No one answered her tenative knock and, impulsively, she tried the door. It swung open when she turned the handle and, after a moment of indecision, she went inside.

The place looked a mess. A thick layer of dust covered the furniture, and stale cigarette smoke cloyed the air. In the small kitchen the dirty dishes filled the sink and overflowed on to the cupboards. Liz had never seen anything like it before, and every instinct within her cried out for her to do something about it.

'I might as well start somewhere,' she told herself grimly and, putting down her handbag, she tapped water into the sink, found a bottle of liquid soap in the windowsill, and waded her way through the pile of dishes.

An hour later there was still no sign of Grant, but Liz had restored a certain amount of order to the kitchen, and the small lounge looked more presentable without its coating of dust, and ashtrays filled with cigarette butts. She felt a bit edgy at invading Grant's privacy in this manner, but she would never have forgiven herself had she turned away and left the cottage in the chaotic state she had found it. She would have thought that Sam Muller would have sent along one of the house servants to do the daily chores for Grant, but then, she supposed, it was none of her business what the arrangement was between Grant and his farm manager.

She found a broom in the closet and swept the kitchen floor. She could not wait for Grant very much longer, but she would leave a note informing him that she had called, and she was still contemplating the wording when a sound behind her made her turn.

Grant stood framed in the kitchen door, his large bulk almost dwarfing it, and one look at his face was enough to tell her that he was in no mood to be pleasant. The stabbing coldness of his steel-grey eyes raked her from head to foot, and she steeled herself for whatever was to follow.

CHAPTER TWO

'How did you get in?' Grant demanded, his harsh voice shattering the awful silence in the small kitchen.

'The door was open,' she replied, quaking inwardly, but outwardly calm as she put the broom away in the closet.

'I shall have to be more careful in future,' he observed cynically, limping towards the table and leaning heavily against it as he demanded icily, 'Why are you here?'

'I had to collect one or two things at the house, so I thought I'd drop in and say hello.'

'It didn't occur to you to leave when you found no one here, I suppose?'

'It did, actually,' she confessed guiltily, 'but it looked as though you could do with a little assistance.'

'So you stayed and carried out your charitable deed for the day.'

His sarcasm stung, but she did not evade his piercing glance. 'If you want to look at it in that light, then . . . yes.'

'I suppose it would be expecting too much to presume that you're on your way out?'

Any other girl would have fled at this point, for Grant could not have made it more clear that she was unwelcome, but Liz merely leaned back against the cupboard and studied him in silence before she said thoughtfully, 'You really have become nasty, haven't you?'

25

'I came here for peace, quiet, and obscurity,' he bit out the words, straightening to his full height, and towering menacingly over her in the process.

'You don't have to tell me why you came to High Ridges,' she retorted sharply. 'You haven't been here for years, but you've finally crawled back into your lair, a wounded animal intent upon licking your scars, and having a grand time feeling sorry for yourself.'

'That's enough!'

His eyes flashed a warning, but she was too angry now to care. 'If the truth hurts, then don't you think it's time you faced up to it?'

'*Get out!*'

'You disappoint me, Grant,' she said quietly, her hands surprisingly steady when she picked up her handbag and slid the strap across her shoulder. 'You always had my admiration and respect for being such a solid, sensible person, but it seems my sentiments have been misplaced.'

Liz was totally unaware of the effect her words might have had on him, or whether, in fact, they had had any effect at all, for she brushed past him, and with her head held high, she walked out of his cottage and into the sunshine. He could go to the devil! she decided, her soft, generous mouth tightening as she climbed into the station-wagon and slammed the door behind her with unnecessary force. If he was so utterly determined to be left alone, then she would jolly well leave him alone in future! Why should she care after all?

That evening, when her anger had simmered, Liz felt more than a little ashamed of herself. She supposed that some of those things had had to be said, but why did *she* have to be the one to say them? She had no desire to hurt him, but neither could she let him continue shutting himself away like some dreary recluse. Could she?

'What's the matter, lass?' Angus demanded when they had coffee in the living-room later that evening. 'You've been rather quiet all through dinner.'

Stacy pushed a tired hand through her short, fair curls, and intervened teasingly, 'What's the bet that it has something to do with Grant Battersby?'

'*Och,* that man,' Angus frowned, his accent more pronounced in moments of anger, or stress. 'He was a fool to cling to that Cavendish woman all these years, and she certainly showed her true colours when that accident shattered his career as a surgeon.'

Liz stared down into her half empty cup and was surprised to discover that her hands were trembling. 'Do you think it's possible that he might never operate again?'

'Never is a long, long time. Who knows what the future has in store for us all,' Angus smiled at her, then he studied her more closely. 'Why this concern for Dr Battersby?'

'When I think of what he used to be, and what he is now, then I can't help being concerned.'

'You haven't still got a crush on him, have you?' Stacy intervened, and when Liz's startled glance met hers, she added quickly, 'You hid it very well, but I was in the throes of falling in love myself at the time, and I recognised the signs in you whenever Grant was about.'

'Oh, lord!' Liz groaned, her cheeks growing pink. 'I hope——'

'No one guessed, I'm sure of that,' Stacy interrupted, 'and if I ever happen to meet Grant during his stay at High Ridges, then you can be sure I shan't tell him.'

'It wouldn't really matter.' Liz put down her cup and met her sister's steady, enquiring gaze. 'I told him myself.'

'You did *what*?' Stacy gasped in surprise, but Angus merely laughed loudly from deep within his strong throat.

'I bet you told him in such a way that he's quite positive you were not telling the truth,' Angus assumed shrewdly, and his infectious laughter soon had them all giggling about the incident.

Liz felt much better after that, but she was hardly in bed that evening when Stacy entered her room after a brief knock on the door.

'I know you're tired,' Stacy began, seating herself on the bed beside Liz, 'but I must have a serious chat with you.'

'This is quite like old times,' Liz laughed lightly, sitting up in bed and flicking her shoulder-length hair away from her face. 'What's on your mind?'

'Don't get involved with Grant Battersby,' Stacy came straight to the point. 'I know him better than you think, and you're bound to be hurt in the process.'

'Why are you telling me this?' Liz asked cautiously, lowering her eyes to the woven blanket on the bed.

'I may be mistaken, but I sense that you still have some feeling left for him, and . . .' her hand gripped Liz's, 'believe me, my dear, you're the one who's going to be hurt. Leave him to women like Myra Cavendish who have ice in their veins. They're the ones who know how to cope, but you, Liz, are all heart beneath that outspoken, often cheeky façade, and you're the kind who would end up suffering the consequences of tangling with a man who'll never know how to give his heart and soul to a woman.'

Stacy went out as quietly as she had come in, and Liz leaned back against the pillows with a tightness in her chest which she could not explain to herself. What Stacy had said made sense, but it did not make pleasant listening when it concerned the man who had held a special place in Liz's heart all these years. What was it, then, that had held him and Myra together for such a long time if it had not been love? Surely the reason for his embittered disposition was because Myra's rejection of him had cut deep into his soul?

Liz was too tired to think. It had been a long day, and her mind was whirling round in senseless circles, so she put out the light and went to sleep.

Stacy went into the nursing home a few days later and, after spending half the night at her side, Angus burst into the house just before breakfast with his coppery hair awry, and his jaw badly in need of a shave.

'It's a bonny wee lass!' he boomed excitedly. 'And she's the spitting image of her mother.'

'I thought it was going to be a boy,' Liz mocked him gently.

'Och,' he grinned, his face colouring slightly, 'there's always a next time.'

'Well, congratulations anyway,' Liz laughed happily, kissing him on his rough cheek, and suffering his bear hug without complaint. 'When am I going to be allowed to see them?'

'This afternoon, of course,' said Angus at once. 'I'll take you there myself.'

He left her standing there in the kitchen, and she heard him whistling loudly as he bounded up the stairs. He was like an overgrown boy, she thought, a smile plucking at the corners of her mouth, and it was this endearing quality of his that had made it so easy to accept him into the family.

Stacy's little girl was exactly as Angus had described her, Liz discovered that afternoon. She was indeed a 'bonny wee lass', and the spitting image of her mother, as Angus had said.

'We're going to call her Rosalie,' Stacy said excitedly, and almost in the same breath she added: 'I hope you won't mind feeding my brute of a husband while I'm lying here incapacitated?'

Liz laughed and shook her head. 'I won't mind at all.'

She did not stay too long at the nursing home. She felt very much like an intruder into their cocoon of happiness, and she envied them somehow when she became aware of that empty void in her own life. She very much wanted a husband and children of her own, but no one, as yet, had quickened her interests in that respect, except . . .! She shook herself free of these disturbing thoughts and, armed with a list, she did the round of the shops. Angus possessed a healthy appetite, and she wanted to cook something special for that evening as a sort of a celebration. They did, after all, have something wonderful to celebrate.

Liz was on her way back to the house when a white Jaguar purred to a halt beside her, and she almost dropped her parcels when the door on the passenger side was flung open and Grant's voice said harshly, 'Get in!'

She hesitated only a brief second before she got in beside him, and her parcels were swiftly transferred to the back seat before he pulled away from the curb.

'Where can we talk privately?' he asked morosely.

'At Stacy's house,' she replied after a quick, nervous glance in his direction. 'There's no one there now, and we'll be absolutely private.'

He asked for the address, and she gave it to him, but they did not speak again until they reached the house. Grant refused her invitation to come in, so she took her parcels into the house and joined him moments later where he waited for her on a bench in a shady spot of the garden.

'Liz . . .' he began, frowning down at the cigarette between his fingers when she sat down beside him, but she interrupted him hastily.

'If you're going to apologise, then please don't. I'm the one who should be apologising for the terrible things I said.'

She felt considerably better after having got that off her chest, but there was a hint of mockery in the eyes that held hers captive as he murmured questioningly, 'Liz, the horror?'

She coloured with embarrassment. 'I've always been a horror where my tongue is concerned, and I have grave doubts whether I shall ever change.'

'One thing I must say for you, Liz,' he laughed shortly. 'No one will ever be left in any doubt as to where they stand with you. You mocked me once when I had a thing going for Pamela, and you ridiculed me mercilessly when I met up with Myra Cavendish.' His mouth twisted cynically. 'You said, if I remember correctly, that Pamela might break my heart a little, but Myra would tear it right out and have it for breakfast.'

'Was I right?' His face hardened, and she added swiftly and apologetically, 'Don't answer that if you don't want to.'

'You were right,' he admitted harshly.

'I'm sorry.'

'Are you?'

He observed her intently when at last she replied with compassion and sincerity, 'To say "I told you so" is petty, and most especially when someone has been hurt.'

'Will you come out to High Ridges again?'

Liz's hands fluttered in her lap, and she gripped them together tightly as she slanted a faintly mocking glance at him. 'Is this an invitation or a challenge?'

'Both,' he said abruptly, his eyes flickering strangely.

'An invitation can be turned down, but I've never been able to resist a challenge.'

He smiled faintly, dropping his cigarette on to the grass and crushing it beneath the heel of his expensive shoe. 'You're an odd child.'

'Not so much of the child, thank you,' she retorted at once. 'I'm twenty-two, remember?'

'It's rather difficult thinking of you as a young woman at a marriageable age when the various stages of your growing up are still so vivid in my memory.'

Liz sighed mockingly. 'That's the problem with family and friends. They never allow you to grow up.'

Grant leaned towards her, and he was suddenly so close that she could see the little creases around his eyes and smell the muskiness of his masculine cologne. It affected her strangely, and so did the deep timbre of his voice when he asked, 'Am I your friend, Liz?'

'We've had our differences in the past, but I would like to think that you're still my friend.'

There was an odd fluttering in her throat, and his finger left a trail of fire against her skin when he traced the curved line of her cheek down to her chin. His light touch had aroused such disturbing sensations that she had almost flinched away from it, but somehow she had managed to remain perfectly still until he had withdrawn his hand.

'When you have nothing better to do I shall welcome your company out at High Ridges,' Grant informed her, and a few minutes later she was watching him drive away.

Liz should have felt elated, but instead she was nervous and troubled. Stacy's warning was still too fresh in her mind to shrug it off, and she recalled some of it now in painful detail. 'Don't get involved with Grant Battersby, you're bound to be hurt in the process. Leave him to women like Myra Cavendish, or end up suffering the consequences of tangling with a man who'll never know how to give his heart and soul to a woman.'

She went into the house to start dinner, but four words swivelled continuously through her mind. *'Don't tangle with Grant!'*

It was too late, she had tangled with him already, and by accepting his challenging invitation she had sealed her fate as securely as if she had padlocked it and thrown away the key. Liz squirmed inwardly at the thought, but she had never been a coward, and she felt certain that she could cope with whatever situation arose.

Almost a week passed before Liz had the opportunity to take a drive out to High Ridges, and a troubled frown creased Stacy's smooth brow when Liz told her where she was going.

'I hope you know what you're doing, Liz,' she said, turning away from the cradle and accompanying Liz into the hall.

'I'm aware of the dangers involved, and I shall, naturally, be on my guard.'

'Being on your guard is not enough,' Stacy warned. 'You'll need armour plating around your heart to be able to deal with Grant.'

'Don't tell me you fell for him once too?' Liz teased.

'I'm not blind, and neither am I senseless,' Stacy said crossly. 'He's a very attractive man with a masculine virility which is potent enough to knock any girl sideways.'

'You haven't seen him since his return to High Ridges, have you?'

'No, I haven't, but——'

'He's lost weight, and he looks ten years older than he actually is,' Liz interrupted defensively. 'He walks with the aid of a stick, and his hand is badly scarred. How badly I don't know yet, but I'll find out in due course.'

'You're feeling sorry for him,' Stacy accused incredulously.

'The word "sorry" is a chilly adjective which pops off the tongue when we accidentally bump into someone,' Liz smiled when they stepped out into the driveway where the station-wagon was parked. 'I prefer the word "compassion". It has more warmth and depth to it.'

'Oh, Liz!' Stacy sighed exasperatedly.

'Take heart, dear sister,' Liz laughed mischievously. 'I haven't fallen foul yet.'

The drive out to High Ridges took less than a half hour, but when she arrived at Grant's cottage it looked very much as if no one was there. The windows were tightly shut and the curtains drawn, and if it had not been for the sleek Jaguar parked in the car-port Liz would have thought he had gone away.

She had been too nervous on her previous visit to take in much, but on this occasion she noticed the small, unfenced garden with its smooth laws and flowering shrubs. A table and a garden bench stood beneath a shady tree, and a little distance away the sparrows were splashing about in a bird bath. It was a warm day with hardly a breeze, and the peaceful serenity of the spot Grant had chosen for his cottage seemed to enfold Liz, calming those fluttering little nerves at the pit of her stomach.

She knocked on the door, quite convinced that Grant had gone out for a walk, but the door was flung open moments later, and her heart almost plummeted to her feet when she found herself staring up into his thunderous face.

'Liz!' he uttered her name in surprise, his brow clearing somewhat, then those steel-grey eyes raked her from head to foot as if he could not quite decide what to do with her.

'Do I come in, or do I park myself on the doorstep?' she asked brightly, wrinkling her nose unobtrusively at the stale cigarette smell that drifted out towards her.

'I think we'd better sit out there in the shade,' he gestured towards the garden bench.

'No need for three guesses to know the reason why,' she grinned meaningfully. 'Why don't you ask Sam Muller to send someone along to do the daily chores for you?'

'I don't want to be bothered with someone fussing about the place.'

'What about your meals?' she asked when they were seated on the wooden bench with a comfortable distance separating them.

'I have a lot of tinned stuff in the cupboards.'

Liz studied him openly, taking in the hollows in his cheeks, and the way his blue shirt hung limply about his wide shoulders. 'No wonder your clothes sit on you as if you were a hanger!'

He glanced at her sharply. 'Do I look that bad?'

'I do believe I've glimpsed a spark of male vanity,' she laughed softly, taking note of the fact that his shirt and pants looked as if they could do with a wash and a hot iron.

'Would that be a good thing, or bad?' he questioned with a speculative gleam in his eyes.

'Good for you at the moment, but bad if you suffered from an overdose,' she replied promptly.

'What would you prescribe, Dr Holden?' he mocked her.

'Oh, nothing unpleasant, Dr Battersby,' she assured him in a similar vein. 'I would say you need plenty of fresh air indoors and out, one good meal a day, and a little less inhalation of dust and nicotine.'

His mouth twitched, but his expression remained severe. 'That sounds wonderful, but who would supply most of what you've just prescribed?'

'That's a bit of a problem,' she admitted.

'What about you?'

'I might.' She cast him a swift, humorous glance. 'On a strictly professional basis, of course.'

'Oh, of course,' he agreed seriously, but his eyes were mocking her in a way that sent a faint rush of colour into her cheeks.

'That's settled, then,' she said abruptly, flicking a beetle off her skirt.

'Is it?'

'Well, isn't it?' she asked, her gaze unfaltering as it met his.

This time it was Grant who looked away, and he took his time lighting a cigarette before he spoke. 'I'd like to accept your very generous offer, but——'

'Don't tell me you're concerned about what people might say?' she interrupted a little incredulously.

'Aren't you?'

'Not in the least,' she answered promptly, but she could imagine what Stacy would have to say about it.

'Your reputation——'

'My reputation is dependent on my conscience, and if my conscience is clear then I have nothing to worry about.'

'Your brand of logic frightens me,' he admitted, blowing twin jets of smoke from his nostrils.

'Nothing ever frightens the great Dr Grant Battersby,' she announced grandly, but he shook his head and studied the tip of his cigarette intently.

'Not so much of the "great", and the "Dr" has now become no more than a courtesy title.'

It felt as though something had taken her heart and was squeezing it painfully, but her voice was sharp when she said: 'I've never known you to be fatalistic about things.'

'Time and circumstances mould and change one.'

'To a certain extent, perhaps, but it doesn't make a healthy-minded man like yourself sit back and say, "Oh, well, let the world crash about my ears and see if I care".'

He laughed shortly, but it had a ring of bitterness to it which her sensitive ears were quick to pick up. 'How do I fight back against the fact that my career is at an end?'

'Who told you that?' she snapped out the question.

'It wasn't necessary for anyone to tell me,' he stated harshly. 'I'm a surgeon, I knew the extent of my injuries, and I knew the implications.'

'And that, you decided, was that!' she bit out the words sarcastically.

'Dammit, Liz!' Grant turned on her with all the pain and fury of hell itself in his eyes. 'I can't even hold a dinner knife properly, let alone a scalpel!'

'At the moment, yes,' she agreed, undaunted, 'but who knows what might happen if you exercised your hand regularly.'

Grant flung his cigarette to the ground and crushed it beneath the heel of his canvas shoe, and there was a hint of violence in the way he did it. 'I suggest we change the subject.'

'Certainly,' she agreed abruptly, and she grasped at once at the first thing that came to mind. 'I never told you, but Stacy had a daughter last week on the very day you gave me a lift home from town, and they've named her Rosalie.'

'How nice,' he growled fiercely.

'You would look much nicer if you didn't scowl,' she rebuked him fearlessly. 'And you might show a little more interest in the fact that I've just become an aunt.'

He sighed heavily and lit another cigarette. 'I'm sure . . . er . . . Rosalie is a charming infant, but she doesn't know what's in store for her with someone like you for an aunt.'

'Now that's what I call loyalty to one's friends,' Liz rebuked him laughingly.

'Stacy and Angus would have apoplexy if you encouraged their daughter into some of the mischief you indulged in as a child,' he verbally underlined his statement.

'I would never dream of encouraging Rosalie to climb trees, and so on,' Liz assured him with mock severity.

'The climbing of trees is bad enough, but it's the "and so on" that horrifies me.'

The laughter left her eyes when she met his cool appraisal. 'Was I really that terrible?'

'It amazes me that you're still in one piece when I think of all the willow tree branches you snapped while imitating Tarzan,' he told her with sardonic humour lurking in his eyes. 'And what about the time you decided to become a bullfighter? If my memory serves me correctly you taunted your father's prize bull into a frothing rage that sent you flying over the fence.'

'I broke my collarbone in that little stunt,' she recalled soberly.

'I'm surprised you didn't break your neck,' he barked disapprovingly, and Liz smiled impishly.

'I'm pretty resilient, you know.'

'I don't doubt it.'

'I also happen to be very thirsty,' she continued without embarrassment. 'Does your hospitality extend to a cup of tea, or something?'

'There's cold beer in the refrigerator.'

'Heaven forbid!' she exclaimed in mock horror.

'You might find a packet of tea in one of the cupboards,' he relented frowningly, 'but I doubt if any of the cups are clean.'

'I can quite believe that,' Liz thought, but aloud she said: 'If I do happen to run across that elusive packet of tea, would you like a cup?'

He adopted a long-suffering expression. 'If I can't

have a cold beer, then I suppose I shall have to settle for tea.'

'Now you're being sensible,' she laughed, getting to her feet and going into the cottage.

With the curtains drawn the rooms looked dark and dismal, and the kitchen was in a similar state to the one she had found it in before. Dirty cups and plates and cutlery littered the cupboards and the sink, but before she could do anything about it she had to find the tea. After a brief search she found it shoved right to the back in one of the cupboards, and while the kettle was boiling she quickly washed the dishes, leaving them on the rack to dry themselves. There was not much else she could do in the time allotted to her, but she fully intended restoring everything to its proper order the following day.

Liz carried the tray of tea out into the garden some minutes later and poured out two cups. She was aware of Grant's eyes following every move she made, but she was not in the least disturbed by it.

'Why did you sell Riverside?' Grant asked while they were drinking their tea. 'Was it necessary, or was it simply that you have no interest in farming?'

'It was a little bit of both,' she confessed, draining her cup and placing it on the tray. 'My father wasn't well these last few years, and he had neither the energy nor the means with which to fight the last two years of severe drought. A large number of our cattle died, and the rest weren't fit for human consumption.'

'So you decided to sell.'

She sensed an accusation in his remark, and said defensively, 'It wasn't an easy decision, but I knew it would take someone far more enterprising than myself to put Riverside back on the map as one of the best cattle ranches in the district.'

'And now you're a lady of leisure.'

'Not exactly,' she denied his mocking statement. 'I write children's stories.'

'Do they sell?'

'They do,' she said firmly, casting a swift glance in his direction. 'And don't look so sceptical about it.'

'Forgive me,' he smiled derisively, 'but I simply can't imagine you churning out stories for children as a paying proposition.'

'It pays well enough,' she replied stiffly, and on the defensive once more.

'Not well enough, I gather, to have saved Riverside.'

'Unfortunately not.' He seemed to be accusing her again, and this time her temper flared. 'Dammit, Grant, if you think I enjoyed having to sell——'

'Temper, temper!' he interrupted mockingly, grabbing a handful of her hair playfully, and twisting it about his fingers, then he leaned closer to examine it. 'Your hair's like spun gold.'

'You're hurting me,' she protested, his nearness definitely disturbing the rhythm of her heart, but he did at least slacken his hold to ease the pressure on her scalp.

'What would you do if I kissed you?' he asked softly, his eyes lingering on her soft mouth in a purposeful way that filled her with panic, but she forcibly suppressed her fears.

'I'd probably run like a scared rabbit,' she said, watching a flicker of surprise dart across his face.

'Does the thought of being kissed frighten you that much?'

'Kissing is a serious business, and it shouldn't be indulged in as if it were casual entertainment.'

'Is that what you think I'm after?' he asked, a dangerous glitter in his eyes.

'Well, you wouldn't want me to think that you have any serious intentions where I'm concerned, would you?' she countered swiftly in her defence.

'You certainly have a refreshing way of dampening a man's ardour,' he laughed harshly, releasing his grip on her hair to light a cigarette. 'Are you always this frank, or do you reserve that for when you're in a tight corner?'

Her heartbeats slowly settled back into their normal rhythm. 'You should know that I have a nasty habit of saying what I think.'

'How could I have forgotten?' he murmured mockingly.

It was time to terminate her visit, Liz decided, getting to her feet and picking up the tray. 'I'll take these cups inside and tidy the kitchen before I leave,' she said without looking at him. 'But you'll have to make do with tinned food until tomorrow.'

'Liz . . .'

'I'll collect a few things on my way out here in the morning, and I shall present you with the dockets,' she went on determinedly as if he had not spoken, but Grant was equally determined to be heard.

'Are you sure that that's what you want to do?'

Her steady, challenging glance met his. 'You're not going to try and stop me, are you?'

'The thought of a juicy steak with fresh vegetables does somehow appeal,' he smiled twistedly.

'I shall keep that in mind,' Liz laughed softly, and a few minutes later she was happily planning the menu for the following day while she swept and tidied the kitchen.

CHAPTER THREE

'YOU'RE crazy!' Stacy's angry voice echoed through the silent living-room. 'Grant Battersby could afford to hire a dozen or more servants without his bank balance even being aware of it, but you politely step in and offer yourself as a willing slave.'

Liz felt her insides contract. 'I have no intention of accepting money from him.'

'Whether you accept money from him or not is quite irrelevant,' Stacy argued. 'Can you imagine what people will say?'

'I can't turn my back on someone who needs help, and Grant needs it badly.'

'Oh, Liz!' Stacy threw up her hands in a gesture of despair. 'You've always been impossible and impulsive, but this is the craziest thing you've ever done!'

'Now hang on there a minute, Stacy,' Angus intervened for the first time. 'I had an interesting chat with Sam Muller yesterday, and from our conversation I gathered that Grant is pretty embittered. If anyone can help him in that respect, then I believe Liz can.'

'Thank you, Angus,' Liz smiled at him gratefully, but Stacy was still not convinced.

'I agree that Liz is capable of shaking the very devil out of his horns, but——'

'Stop worrying so much, my love,' Angus interrupted his wife. 'Liz can take care of herself.'

It was gratifying to know that Angus, at least, had faith in her, and Liz appreciated his support when she had needed it most. She could not, of course, explain to herself why she felt this urgent desire to help Grant, but she told herself that it was the least she could do for someone who had been a friend of the family for so many years. There could be no other explanation, could there?

Liz arrived at Grant's cottage shortly after nine the following morning. The door was unlocked, but Grant was out, so she packed away the things she had brought with her, and tidied the kitchen. In the bathroom she discovered that he had made some attempt, at least, to wash his clothes, so she finished the job for him and thrust the whole lot into the tumble drier.

She worked quickly, dusting, sweeping, and opening up the windows as she went along to let in the fresh air. Two hours later, when she was in the kitchen peeling the vegetables, and preparing the steak, she saw Grant approaching the cottage, and she switched on the kettle to make a pot of tea.

He was walking slowly, pausing occasionally to rest, and Liz had made the tea and was ready to pour when he finally entered the cottage through the kitchen door.

'Would you like a cup?' she asked, skipping the usual preliminaries, and he nodded briefly, lowering himself on to the upright wooden chair beside the table.

'How did Stacy react to this decision of yours?' he asked unexpectedly.

'She thought I was crazy,' Liz said without turning.

'I imagined she'd talk you out of it.'

Something in his voice made her turn to glance at him speculatively. 'Don't tell me you were actually hoping she would succeed?'

'I was,' he stated bluntly.

Liz was strangely hurt, but she hid it behind a laugh. 'You're an ungrateful so-and-so, aren't you?'

'I prefer my own company at the moment.'

'Oh, but you're welcome to it,' she snapped at him, picking up his cup of tea and marching towards the door. 'You may have your tea in the lounge, *sir*, while I get on with preparing your meal.'

'Liz . . .' With an agility she had not expected of him, he barred her way, and those compelling grey eyes held hers masterfully. 'Strange as it may seem to you, it's you I'm thinking of.'

'Really?'

'Your reputation, for one thing, is not going to be worth much when word gets around that you're here most mornings,' he said, ignoring her sarcasm. 'And for another, I'm bound to be foul company most of the time.'

'Your foul moods shan't bother me, and my reputation is my concern, not yours.'

His mouth tightened. 'I'd rather have people thinking of you as Liz the horror, and not Liz the——'

'Don't use that word!' she interrupted sharply, and the hand that held the cup was shaking visibly. 'If people don't know me well enough by now to realise that I could never be that kind of woman, then they're not worth bothering about.' There was a hint of defiance in her golden-brown eyes, and her voice was businesslike as she asked, 'Where do you want your tea? Here, or in the lounge?'

'Here, where I can watch you,' Grant smiled faintly, resuming his seat, and she put his cup down on the table with a disgusted snort.

'Are you afraid that I might walk away with the family silver?'

'The family silver, as you call it, is at my home in Johannesburg,' he told her mockingly. 'It's a precaution I took even before Sam Muller moved into the house.'

'It seems I shall have to forget my "get rich quick" notions,' she sighed with mock disappointment, picking up a potato and peeling it energetically.

'Is money important to you?'

'Don't be ridiculous!' she laughed, startled by the severity of his tone.

'What if it could have prevented the sale of Riverside?' he persisted harshly, and Liz put down the potato before turning to face him.

'That's a tantalising question,' she said gravely.

'Do I get an answer to it?'

'You're being unfair, and you know that, but——'. She bit her lip thoughtfully. 'I admit that money was important to me a few months ago. It would have saved us all a lot of heartache if I could have afforded to install a manager as you've done here at High Ridges, but there was no way I could lay my hands on that sort of capital, so we decided to make a clean break, and sell.' She shrugged carelessly. 'Money lost its importance to me after that.'

Grant drank his tea, and Liz resumed peeling the potatoes, convinced that the subject was at an end, then he surprised her by saying, 'You must have made quite a lot out of the sale.'

'Oh, yes,' she smiled mockingly. 'After all the accounts, I.O.U.s and whatnots had been paid, the three Holden girls are in a position to say that they have a little nest-egg which will still necessitate working for the rest of our lives.'

'But your father——'

'Was *once* one of the wealthiest farmers in the district,' she forestalled him without bitterness or rancour.

'What happened?'

'I told you,' she replied vaguely, wiping her hands on a cloth, and swallowing down a mouthful of her cold tea. 'There was the drought, and he wasn't well.'

Grant's eyes narrowed perceptibly. 'You're hiding something from me.'

Liz was on the verge of telling him to mind his own business when she realised that, if she wanted to help him at all, there would have to be complete honesty between them about all things.

'My father started drinking heavily,' she conceded, 'and he subsequently seemed to lose interest in life itself.'

'But why?' Grant frowned.

'I don't know,' Liz gestured helplessly with her hands. 'He seemed to want to dwell in the past, and he talked a lot about my mother.' She bit her lip to steady it while she considered her father's behaviour over the past two years. 'I think he missed my mother more than anyone ever guessed, and perhaps that was one of the reasons he never married again,' she finally explained.

'No one could ever replace her.'

Grant sounded quite strange, and Liz sensed at once that he was not thinking of her mother, but of Myra Cavendish. She glanced at him questioningly, but he averted his eyes, and she was positive now that she had been correct in her assumption.

'When I fell off my horse as a child, my father made me get up and ride again, and that's what life is all about,' she said in a voice which was deliberately devoid of sympathy. 'We take plenty of spills, but we have to get up and go on again.'

'Are you lecturing me?' he asked coldly.

'Could be,' she said abruptly. 'You're very much down at the moment, and you could do with a helping hand into the saddle.'

'Into the saddle of what?' he demanded harshly, his glance suspicious, and his manner somehow forbidding.

'Work, for instance,' she replied without hesitation, 'or simply living.'

'I'm going for a walk,' he thundered, snatching up his stick and getting to his feet.

'Do that,' she said, quite unperturbed by his display of temper. 'The more you exercise that leg, the sooner you'll be walking without a stick.'

'Thanks for the advice, *Dr* Holden,' he snarled at her as he reached the door.

'You're welcome.'

The cottage seemed to shudder with the force of the door being slammed, and Liz flinched, realising for the first time how tense she had been. From the kitchen window she could see him making his arduous way towards the river, and her heart ached for him.

When Liz left the cottage shortly after one o'clock that day she had done the ironing, and Grant's dinner was in the oven. She only hoped he would return before the steak was spoiled.

During the week that followed Liz seldom saw Grant. He left the cottage soon after her arrival, and returned only after she had left. On one particular morning she decided that she had had enough of this, and she deliberately stepped into his path.

'You can't avoid me for ever, you know,' she said.

'Or do you intend never to speak to me again?'

'I'm following your advice, and exercising my leg,' he remarked pointedly, gesturing her out of his way with his stick, but she caught it in her hand and held on to it.

'Grant?' Her golden glance captured his. 'If you would prefer me to stay away altogether, then all you have to do is say so.'

His jaw tightened, and she thought for a moment that he was going to tell her to do just that, then he said abruptly, 'I'm going for a walk, but I'll be back for tea.'

Liz released her grip on his stick, and when he walked away she had a strange feeling that she had won a small victory.

Life took on a different pattern after that. Grant would go for a long walk early in the morning, and would return for tea. Afterwards he would sit with her in the kitchen while she prepared his meal, and they would have lengthy discussions about various topics, but they seldom talked about anything personal. Quite soon, however, Liz was sharing his meal with him each day before returning to Pietersburg, and she began to treasure those moments she shared with him.

Grant was regaining his strength rapidly, the hollows in his cheeks had filled out, and his clothes no longer hung on his frame as though they were several sizes too big for him. His limp was becoming less noticeable, although he still relied on his sturdy stick for support, but the lack of total flexibility in his hand was still something that troubled him immensely.

Liz spent her afternoons and her evenings trying to catch up on her work, but it was becoming increasingly difficult to shut Grant out of her thoughts. Physically he was in better shape than he had been on his arrival, but mentally he was still embittered, frustrated, and cynical. His fits of depression were less frequent, but she sensed that it lurked continuously beneath his often flippant remarks. He treated Liz like a younger sister, and it was to her as if they had gone back to that time when she had been a sixteen-year-old, but she could not in all honesty say that she minded. It became her shield behind which she could hide her feelings, and she was grateful for it, but deep down she was becoming aware of an impatient longing for something more. She thrust this thought aside and concentrated on her work once more, but a few days later she was to recall her thoughts when the situation between Grant and herself altered drastically.

She was standing on a kitchen chair, hanging up the lounge curtains which she had taken down and washed early that morning, when she became aware of someone in the room with her.

'Oh, hello,' she said, casting a quick, casual glance over her shoulder. 'I didn't hear you come in.'

'Can I help in any way?' Grant asked, stepping further into the room.

'You could pass me that curtain draped across the back of that chair when I've finished with this one,' she suggested, and he waited until she had slipped the last hook into place before he passed her the bright floral curtain she had asked for.

She felt her breasts straining against the bodice of her dress when she reached up to hang the curtain, and she was aware, too, that she was displaying perhaps a little too much of her smooth, shapely legs. She knew that Grant was watching her, she could almost feel his eyes acquainting themselves with her feminine curves, and although embarrassment sent a surge of warmth into her cheeks, there was a part of her that actually welcomed his masculine appraisal. Her fingers fumbled nervously with the last few hooks, and then Grant was there, his hands gripping her firmly about the waist as he lifted her effortlessly on to the floor.

Their eyes met, and something in those silver-grey depths deepened the flush on her cheeks. He was looking at her as if he was seeing her for the first time as a woman instead of a child, and she was not sure whether she ought to feel excited or afraid. Young men her own age had flirted with her occasionally, and she had been able to laugh it off and hold them at bay, but she could not do the same with Grant; not with the man who had always held her heart so carelessly in the palm of his hands.

His fingers bit into her slim waist with surprising strength, the heat of his hands burning her flesh through the silk of her dress, and her raised glance settled inadvertently on his mouth. The harsh lines had been softened by a distinct sensuality, and her pulse quickened with a longing so intense that her breath locked in her throat.

With an expertise that should not have surprised her, he moulded her hips to his own with a firm hand in the hollow of her back, and she felt herself trembling when his injured hand found its way into her hair to cup the back of her head and tilt her face up to his. She knew what was going to happen, she could see it in his eyes, and if ever there was a time to break free and run, then it was *now*. Something warned her that she was courting disaster, but her limbs felt as if they had turned to water and, when he lowered his dark head, she did nothing to avoid that warm mouth which was taking possession of hers.

'Too late!' her mind accused when her lips quivered responsively beneath his, but her heart was beating so hard against her ribs that it drowned out whatever else the little voice of her conscience might have said.

Liz had dreamed about this often enough, and there was a time when she had tried to imagine what it would feel like to be kissed by Grant, but never, not even in her wildest dreams, had she imagined this pulsating warmth that leapt through her veins. It felt as if she had imbibed a heady wine, and was becoming intoxicated by it. The scent of his aftershave mingled with that of tobacco, and stirred her senses until she was in no position to resist when the sensual pressure of his mouth parted her inexperienced lips. She had been kissed before, but never had she imagined that a kiss could be so intimate, and her hands slid upwards across his chest to cling tightly to his shoulders when it felt as if the room was spinning crazily about her.

She was experiencing a fiery initiation into the intimacies shared between a man and a woman, and the effect it was having on her emotions was alarming. Those clever hands caressed her, awakening the most primitive fires within her, and she stirred protestingly against him.

Grant released her at once, but she had difficulty in controlling her breathing, and so, it seemed, had he. His pupils had become dilated to the extent that his eyes were almost black, and a fine film of perspiration stood out on his broad forehead and upper lip. He looked disturbed and quite unlike himself, but then neither was she as calm as she would have wanted to be. She could still feel the heat of his body against her own, her scalp tingled where his fingers had lain, and

the intimacy of his kisses and caresses had left her
flushed and awkward.

'I'll put the kettle on for tea,' she said in a voice
which was surprisingly steady, and he did not try to
stop her when she picked up the chair and brushed
past him on her way to the kitchen.

She made the tea and set out the cups, but her mind
was not on what she was doing. She was reliving those
moments in his arms, and she was having difficulty in
coming to terms with the blinding realisation that her
teenage crush had stood the test of time to develop
into a deep and lasting devotion. Why it should have
surprised her she could not say, but it did.

'Liz . . .' She swung round nervously at the sound of
Grant's deep voice. 'About what happened just now. I
wouldn't want you to think that——'

'That you have any serious intentions where I'm
concerned?' she interrupted him swiftly, and hid her
hurt behind a laugh when the look on his face told her
that she had hit the centre target. 'Good heavens,
Grant, I'm not that naïve. You kissed me on the spur
of the moment, and so what!'

He smiled twistedly. 'I'm relieved that you see it in
that light.'

She poured his tea and placed his cup before him.
She felt very much like saying, 'Drink it, and I hope it
scalds your mouth, or chokes you!' But instead she
remained silent, and left him there in the kitchen while
she went through to the bathroom to check on the
items of clothing she had left to soak in the bath.

Liz tried to behave as if nothing unusual had
happened, but during the rest of that morning, *and* the
next, she was aware of Grant's brooding glances following her wherever she went. For the first time in

her life she felt nervous and edgy, as if something was brewing, but she was determined not to shy away from it.

'Must you leave now?' Grant asked when they had finished their meal and the kitchen had been tidied.

'I haven't an appointment elsewhere, if that's what you mean,' she replied cautiously.

'Shall we go for a walk?'

She was faintly surprised at his suggestion, but she said at once, 'If you like.'

They took his favourite path down to the grassy verge of the river, walking in silence, and taking care not to touch each other. It was a hot day with not even a breeze stirring the silent veld, and birds and insects alike seemed to seek refuge from the scorching sun.

Grant paused beneath a shady willow and they stood facing each other a little awkwardly beside the slow-moving river. His brooding glance travelled over her, taking in the golden sheen of her hair which framed her small, pointed face, and then his eyes slid down to linger on the gentle curves of her youthful figure. She felt the heat of his eyes on her body like a physical touch, and her pulse rate quickened, choking off her breath. His eyes were seducing her, tearing at her defences, and making her aware of his virile masculinity to the extent that she quivered on the brink of an aching yet unfamiliar need.

'Stop looking at me like that, Grant,' she managed at last when his glance lingered with purposeful intent on her soft, generous mouth.

'Like what?' he queried mockingly.

'As if you're hatching some devious plot with me in mind.'

He laughed shortly, strong white teeth flashing and

contrasting heavily with his tanned features, and there was a curious light in his eyes when he asked, 'Is that how I've been looking at you?'

'You know you have, and you've been doing so ever since——'

'Ever since I kissed you yesterday?' he filled in for her when she paused abruptly. Liz nodded, too embarrassed to speak, and his eyes glittered strangely when he said: 'I haven't been able to forget what you felt like in my arms. You felt so small and soft, and you were so very responsive.'

'Shut up!' she snapped, her cheeks flaming.

'I never thought I would ever see you blush,' he teased with a faintly derisive smile curving his mouth, and when his hands framed her heated face that strange weakness invaded her limbs once again.

He lowered his head, and his breath mingled with hers before their lips met. His kisses were light, and explorative, as if he were sampling her lips and trying to decide whether he liked the taste, and Liz stood perfectly still, enduring his tantalising kisses with her hands clenched tightly at her sides. She found it a tremendous effort not to respond, and not to give in to the desire to drag his head down to deepen their kiss, but she was determined to resist him.

Grant laughed softly against her mouth, and she knew with startling clarity that he was fully aware of her desperate efforts to remain detached. She raised her hands in anger, intending to thrust him from her, but he seemed to anticipate her move, and she found herself held captive in the hard circle of his arms. She was strong despite her size, but she could not break his hold, and his intimate invasion of her mouth sapped her energy. That intoxicating warmth invaded her body once more, and she melted shamelessly against his hard, muscled frame. It was so much easier to respond than to resist, and her arms were locked about his neck when he finally lowered her on to the soft grass.

His mouth devoured hers with long, drugging kisses until she could no longer think coherently. She was conscious only of the clean male smell of him, of the almost convulsive movements of his hands against her back, and of the heavy beat of his heart against her own. When his mouth eventually left hers it was to explore the sensitive column of her throat, and to trail a path of fire along her smooth shoulder to where the thin strap of her cotton dress had been brushed aside by his impatient fingers. A thousand little nerves seemed to come alive to his touch, but sanity returned when she felt the heat of his hand through the thin material at her breast.

'Please don't,' she groaned, gripping his wrist tightly and dragging his hand away from her.

Grant raised his head, and the eyes that met hers were dark and stormy with suppressed passion when he grunted, 'What's the matter?'

'We've known each other for a long time, haven't we, Grant?' she asked, succeeding somehow in making her voice sound casual despite the alarming way her pulses continued to react to his nearness.

'We have,' he acknowledged abruptly.

'Long enough for us to be honest with each other?'

'I would say so,' he replied with a derisive smile and amazing tolerance.

'Am I being placed in the category of light entertainment?' she questioned him bluntly, and he released her at once so that she could sit up.

'Is that what you think?' he demanded harshly, his eyes on her hand when it went up to adjust the strap of her dress.

'At this precise moment I don't really know what to think,' Liz confessed quietly, feeling totally miserable as she sat there on the grass beside him.

'You've been kissed before, haven't you?'

'It's not something I've indulged in often, and most certainly not to this extent, and . . .' Her voice wavered precariously, but she pulled herself together and said awkwardly, 'I'm more than just a little out of my depth, Grant.'

'In what way?'

'I'm not like Pamela,' she sighed, pushing her trembling fingers through her long hair and looking everywhere but at him. 'She would know how to deal with a situation such as this, but I don't.'

'Ah, yes,' he murmured, and the mockery in his voice grated along her raw, quivering nerves. 'To you kissing is a serious business, and not to be trifled with.'

'Don't mock me, Grant!' she lashed out at him in a flash of temper. 'And if it's games you want to play, then I suggest you find someone else!'

She leapt to her feet and ran back to the cottage as if the devil himself were after her, and when she drove away from High Ridges minutes later she was in a filthy mood which was quite alien to her nature.

Stacy took one look at Liz when she walked into the house half an hour later, and asked: 'What happened?'

'What makes you think that something happened?' Liz fumed.

'You don't generally rev the car's engine unnecessarily and slam doors,' Stacy explained, eyeing

Liz curiously. 'Did Grant make a pass at you?'

Liz gave her sister a withering look before crossing the hall towards the stairs.

'I received a letter from Pamela this morning.' Liz paused on the second step and turned as Stacy said: 'She added a postscript for you.'

'Did she?' Liz asked cautiously.

'She simply confirms what I've said all along,' Stacy told her.

Liz smiled tightly. 'I don't need a medal for guessing that it has something to do with Grant.'

'I'll read it to you,' said Stacy, taking the letter from the drawer in the hall table and opening it. 'Tell Liz to stay away from Grant. He's deadly,' she read out the words Pamela had scrawled on the thin sheet of paper.

A wave of anger swept through Liz, and it was so intense that she felt like tearing down the house in an effort to relieve it.

'Tell Pamela to mind her own business, and that goes for you too!' she heard her voice echoing shrilly through the silent house, then she was darting up the stairs, taking them two at a time in her haste to get away before Stacy saw the ridiculous tears stinging her eyes.

'Damn, damn, *damn!*' she cursed loudly in the privacy of her room, then she gave way to the tears of frustration and anger.

It was futile wishing that she could be like Pamela. She was Liz the horror, the impossible, the daredevil. She had been afraid of nothing and no one until this afternoon when she had found herself floundering as if in deep, unknown waters. She had wanted to let go, she had wanted the tide to take her where it willed, but she had been afraid. *Afraid!* If those moments had meant nothing to Grant, then they had meant something to her, and she dared not let him make a mockery of her feelings.

An hour later Liz had calmed down sufficiently to apologise to Stacy, but nothing Stacy could say would dissuade her from returning to High Ridges the following morning.

If Liz was surprised to find the cottage looking as if Grant had indulged in a drinking orgy the night before, then he seemed even more surprised to find her there when he returned from his walk later that morning.

'Did you think I wouldn't be coming back?' she asked lightly, switching on the kettle and spooning tea into the pot.

'I must admit I had nightmares of eating out of tins again,' he confessed with a faintly sheepish grin.

'My anger was directed at myself, and not at you.' She cast him an apologetic glance. 'I'm sorry.'

'Now I wonder why you were angry with yourself,' he laughed softly. 'Could it be that underneath that tough exterior of "Liz the Horror" there lurks a frightened young woman?'

He was so close to the truth that only the tight control she had on herself saved her from giving herself away. 'As a child I was afraid of walking down the passage with the darkness behind me, but only until one day when I turned and faced into it.' Her steady gaze met his. 'I learnt a valuable lesson.'

'Are you saying that if you face the things you fear, then you find you have the means with which to conquer your fears?'

'That's about it,' she smiled.

He peered intently into her eyes. 'Do you fear me?'

'No.' The smell of the sun and the bush seemed to cling to him, and it stirred her senses dangerously. 'I fear myself,' she heard herself confessing her vulnerability.

His eyebrows rose in sardonic amusement. 'Now, what am I supposed to make of that?'

'I'll let you know when I've unravelled it for myself,' she promised lightly, avoiding his probing eyes as she concentrated on making the tea.

He did not pursue the subject, but as she went about her usual tasks she found herself colliding repeatedly with Grant, or his brooding glances. It made her jittery, and she eventually had no option but to order him out of the kitchen. He went, but he returned a half hour later with a small bunch of wild yellow daisies, and she observed him unobtrusively while he filled an empty pickle jar with water and thrust the daisies into it.

They had their meal with the bright yellow daisies on the table between them, and there was something about his ridiculous gesture that made her want to laugh and cry simultaneously, but she smothered the feeling forcibly, and concentrated instead on her food.

When they reached the coffee stage the silence between them became oddly strained, and Liz was suddenly in a hurry to get away. She drank her coffee as quickly as possible, then stacked the dishes into the small sink. She tapped water on to the plates, and squeezed detergent into it, but all the while she was conscious of Grant watching her intently.

It was more than just unnerving, she thought furiously when she was elbow-deep in the soapsuds, but if he had something on his mind, then it was up to him to speak.

Was he thinking of Myra Cavendish? Liz felt chilled. Perhaps he was wishing that Myra was here, washing his dishes, sweeping his floors, cooking his food, and although Liz found it hilarious trying to imagine the glamorous Myra doing those chores, she could not ignore that painful little stab in the region of her heart.

'Would you make me a fresh cup of coffee before you go, and bring it to the lounge?' Grant's voice interrupted her disturbing thoughts, and she glanced at him over her shoulder with a slightly guilty start as if she was certain he had somehow penetrated her thoughts.

'Yes, of course,' she heard herself saying, but she was speaking to an empty kitchen, for Grant was already walking down the short passage towards the lounge.

Liz worked swiftly, washing, drying, packing away, and when she finally stood with Grant's cup of coffee in her hands she found herself staring at the daisies he had arranged so haphazardly in the pickle jar. It had made her want to laugh and cry before, but now she felt only like crying and, swallowing down the lump in her throat, she went through to the lounge to give Grant his coffee.

'Don't go yet,' he said when she turned to leave. 'I've been thinking a great deal these past few days.'

Liz stood immobile, her hands jammed into the pockets of her wide skirt to hide the fact that they were shaking. 'He's going away,' she thought bitterly. She had lived through a lifetime of Grant walking in and out of her life, but this would be the last time their paths would cross, for the agony of saying goodbye had reached its peak.

His cup of coffee stood untouched on the table

beside his chair, and she stared down into those shut-
tered eyes, steeling herself for whatever it was he was
going to say.

'Will you marry me, Liz?'

CHAPTER FOUR

IT took several heart-stopping seconds for his words to penetrate the protective armour she had placed around her mind. 'Will you marry me, Liz?' he had said in a cold, dispassionate voice, and for one mind-jarring moment she was not sure whether to laugh, cry, or scream abuse at him. He was joking, of course. He could not possibly be asking her to become his wife, could he?

There was no sign of laughter on those rigidly handsome features, only the quiet, brooding look of a man who was waiting with remarkable patience for an answer to his emotionless proposal, and anger replaced the numbness of shock.

'I'm told a proposal of marriage is normally preceded by a declaration of love,' she informed him with mocking derision, and he had the grace to look faintly uncomfortable.

'I haven't any love to offer you, but I do need a wife.'

'What you're actually saying is that you need a woman in your bed,' she stated bluntly.

'Is that so terrible?'

'Yes ... and no.' She turned away from him and stared out of the window at the small sunlit garden beyond. Everything looked so blessedly normal out there in comparison with the wild confusion raging inside of her. Her throat felt tight, and her face felt stiff with the effort to control her expression. 'Why me, Grant?' she finally asked without turning. 'Why me?'

'You're lively company, you're a good cook, and my shirts have never been ironed so perfectly since you took my clothes to task.'

'I suppose I should feel flattered,' she laughed with a note of faint hysteria in her voice.

'Dammit, Liz, if it's all that romantic nonsense you want, then forget it, but ...' She turned when he paused, and as their eyes met across the room he said: 'I have every reason to believe we'll have a good marriage.'

Liz felt her cheeks grow warm, but she did not look away. 'I presume you're referring to the physical side of marriage?'

'I am.'

She turned away from the mockery in his eyes and said angrily, 'You're not really offering me much, are you? Only physical desire.'

'You'll never want for anything, Liz.'

His voice was low and quiet, but there was a wealth of meaning threaded through that remark, and she rounded on him furiously. 'Do you think I would consider any man's financial status of prime importance?'

'Confound it!' he growled, lighting a cigarette and blowing the smoke forcibly towards the ceiling. 'What do you want, then?'

'I want what you obviously can't give me,' she replied with that direct honesty which was so true to her nature, and this was not the time to hide behind evasive statements, she decided when she looked directly into those steel-grey eyes observing her questioningly. 'I want your love, Grant.'

He looked taken aback, and a strained silence hovered between them before he asked, 'Why is that so important?'

'Because I happen to love you.'

She had spoken those words quietly and calmly, and without hesitation. The secret, so long hidden, was revealed, and if he had doubted her sincerity, then one look into her unwavering eyes would have given him his answer.

'You're nothing if not truthful,' he almost accused her, and she winced inwardly.

'I believe in honesty at all times, no matter how much it may hurt.'

For endless seconds he said nothing while he studied the tip of his cigarette with frowning intensity, then he raised his glance to hers and said roughly, 'I can't give you what I haven't got to give, Liz. I can give you respect, companionship, and the physical side of love, but no more than that.' His mouth twisted into a cynical smile which stabbed painfully at her heart. 'For what it's worth, that's my proposal.'

'I suppose I must be a glutton for punishment,' she smiled unsteadily, making up her mind suddenly despite all the warnings flashing through her brain and, kneeling down at his feet, she said simply, 'I accept.'

Was it relief she saw in his eyes? She could not be sure, but he put out his cigarette and drew her up into his arms. She lost herself in his embrace, and returned his fierce kisses with a warmth that flowed from her heart. She wished this moment would go on for ever, but she realised that nothing lasts for ever when Grant released her much too soon for her liking.

'It's time you went back to the safety of Stacy's home,' he said harshly, his eyes mocking her for her reluctance to leave him. 'We'll discuss all the details tomorrow.'

Liz did not argue with him. She was too happy, and also too agonisingly aware of the fact that she had agreed to marry a man who could never love her the way she loved him.

It was not until after dinner that evening that Liz passed on the news of her intended marriage to Stacy and Angus and, as she had expected, her sister took it badly.

'Have you gone out of your mind?' Stacy demanded, her usually soft voice high-pitched and anxious.

'I love him, Stacy.'

'You're a fool if you imagine he could ever feel the same way about you.'

That hurt; it would always hurt, but Liz dared not let Stacy see it. 'I know he doesn't love me. He made no secret of it, and I accepted his proposal on those terms.'

'What about Myra Cavendish?' Stacy demanded. 'What if she decides to come back into his life?'

A cold hand gripped Liz's heart, but she smiled and announced with dramatic humour, 'I'm hoping that by that time he will have fallen *madly* in love with me.'

'Oh, Liz!' Stacy shook her fair, curly head and glanced briefly at her husband for support. 'Do you know what you're letting yourself in for?'

'I know it isn't going to be easy,' Liz sighed, 'but I'm hoping for the best.'

'Well, if I might interrupt a moment to say something,' said Angus, coming across to where Liz stood clutching her hands so tightly in front of her that they ached. 'Congratulations, Liz,' he smiled, hugging her against him and kissing her on her cool cheek. 'When's the great day to be?'

'We haven't discussed it yet, but I——' She bit her lip and glanced beseechingly at Stacy. 'I presume it will be soon.'

Stacy followed her husband's example, but there was anxiety in her doe-like eyes when she gripped Liz's hands. 'I'm afraid for you.'

'Don't be silly, my love,' Angus laughed comfortably, draping a heavy arm about each of them. 'Liz can take care of herself.'

That night, when Liz lay awake in bed, Angus' words drifted back into her mind. *Liz can take care of herself.* She appreciated his confidence in her, but *was* she capable of taking care of herself? Would her love for Grant not make her more vulnerable under the circumstances?

Liz slept badly that night, in fact she hardly slept at all, and she got up the following morning with a thumping headache which did not abate until she had swallowed a couple of aspirins.

When she arrived at Grant's cottage that morning she found him sitting at the kitchen table with a mug of coffee between his hands. He was dressed in khaki pants and a blue shirt, but his jaw was unshaven, and there were shadows beneath his eyes.

'I decided to skip the exercise this morning,' he answered her silent query.

'Oh.' She studied him more closely. 'You're not ill, are you?'

'I simply didn't sleep too well,' he replied, gesturing her into the chair close to his, and she smiled faintly as she joined him at the table.

'Neither did I have much sleep,' she confessed

quietly, and he glanced at her sharply.

'Have you been doubting your decision?'

'No,' she shook her head and eyed him anxiously. 'Have you?'

He put down his mug and slipped his hand beneath her hair. His fingers caressed the nape of her neck, awakening little nerves that sent shivers of pleasure down her spine, then he drew her head towards him and covered her mouth with his. Their lips clung, tasted, explored, and the intimacy of his kisses made her feel a little dizzy with the emotions he aroused.

'I want you, Liz, and God knows I need you,' he groaned against her mouth. 'We have to talk, and at this rate we're not getting anywhere fast.'

His voice was low and seductive, and she responded to it in a way she had never thought possible, but he was right, they had a lot to discuss. Taking the initiative, she broke his light clasp and sat back in her chair.

'All right, let's talk,' she said unsteadily, trying to behave naturally even though her cheeks were flushed, and her heart was racing at an uncomfortable pace.

'How soon will you marry me?' Grant asked evenly, and she envied him his obvious control.

'As soon as you wish.'

'Saturday?'

Liz felt her heart lurch in her breast. 'That's two days away!'

'We could postpone it, of course, if you want the usual wedding with all the trappings.'

He made the offer, and he would go through with it if she wished, but she sensed somehow that an elaborate wedding did not appeal to him. She was not so sure that she wanted a big wedding herself. With her father not there to take her into the church, and Stacy with a baby barely a few weeks old, it would perhaps not be such a good idea, Liz decided.

'I think a quiet wedding would do nicely, and Saturday will be fine,' she assured him after a thoughtful pause.

'What about your family?' asked Grant, looking oddly relieved.

'They'll agree to whatever we decide.'

His heavy eyebrows rose a fraction. 'There were no objections to the news that you were thinking of marrying me?'

'Stacy thought I'd gone out of my mind, but I'm old enough to make my own decisions,' she brushed aside his query, then she changed the subject quickly. 'We will live here, won't we?'

'For a while, yes.'

'Grant . . .' She hesitated, but the question had to be asked. 'What about Myra?'

His jaw hardened, and his eyes became slivers of ice. 'We won't discuss her.'

'But——'

'I said we won't discuss her!' he interrupted savagely, thrusting back his chair and getting to his feet. 'She belongs in the past, and that's where she'll stay.'

'Very well, if that's what you want,' she replied coldly.

'Liz, please try to understand.'

His hands were shaking when they gripped her shoulders, and then he was drawing her up into his arms, and holding her so tightly that she was finding it difficult to breathe. His cheek was rough against her own, his breath warm against her temple, and then he was kissing her with a fierce hunger that made her numb with a new kind of fear. What was there he wanted her to understand? That he was using her to forget Myra Cavendish? It hurt . . . oh, God, it hurt!

'I think I'd better get on with what I'm supposed to do,' she said at length when her lips were freed from his fiery kisses.

'I'll take a drive into town to make the necessary arrangements.'

'You'd better shave first,' she suggested, her cheek still stinging where his beard had scratched her, and she could not help noticing the scars on the back of his hand when he fingered his jaw.

'I'd better shave,' he agreed, grinning as he walked out of the kitchen and left her clinging limply to the cupboard.

Liz's legs were shaking, and she felt a little sick inside, but she had never lacked confidence, and she was not going to lose her courage. Their marriage was going to succeed, she would make every effort to see that it did, and in time, perhaps, he might learn to love her a little.

Liz went shopping that afternoon for a wedding outfit, and chose an ivory-coloured suit with a wide-brimmed hat to match. It was nothing elaborate, but when she observed herself in the full-length mirror she agreed with the saleslady that she looked cool and chic.

'Is that what you're going to wear on your wedding day?' Stacy asked when she walked into Liz's room that evening and saw the outfit hanging against the wardrobe.

Liz looked up from her work and nodded. 'I thought it would look smart and not too flashy.'

'You'll look lovely in it,' Stacy assured her, fingering the expensive material.

'Do you really think so?'

'You don't need me to tell you that,' Stacy smiled, then she remembered why she was there. 'We have a guest for dinner, so I suggest you put on something nice.'

'Is it someone important?' Liz asked absently, nibbling at her pencil and allowing her mind to drift back to the characters in the story she was attempting to write.

'I'll leave that for you to decide,' Stacy laughed softly. 'And come down as soon as you're ready, will you?'

She went out, closing the door quietly behind her, and Liz sighed irritably. She wanted to get this story in the post before Saturday, and it was difficult enough trying to write while she thought of what still lay ahead of her. If Angus and Stacy were entertaining a guest this evening, then she wished, for once, that they had left her out of their arrangements. She was not exactly in the right mood to be polite to strangers, but for Stacy's sake she supposed she would have to be.

'Put on something nice,' Stacy had said and, studying the dresses hanging in the wardrobe, Liz selected a silky sapphire blue frock which she had worn only once before. It was cool and comfortable, and it added a touch of sophistication to her appearance.

When she observed herself in the mirror some minutes later the words 'fragile and feminine' leapt into her mind, and she giggled to herself. Deep down she would always be a tomboy at heart, but there was one man who had always succeeded in making her intensely aware of her femininity, and soon, very soon, he was going to be her husband.

Husband. The word shook her considerably. Grant would be her possessor, and she the possessed. Body and soul she would be his to do with as he pleased, and thinking about it in those terms suddenly made her nervous and edgy. She had no experience in sexual intimacies; it was something quite a few of her friends had indulged in, but Liz had been rigidly determined to remain untouched, almost as if she had been saving herself for the man she would one day marry. What if, as a result of her inexperience, she failed Grant?

It was a frightening thought, but she thrust it aside for the moment, and went downstairs.

She could hear Stacy in the kitchen, and Angus was in his study presumably chatting to their guest. She would have a few moments alone to control that awful tremor at the pit of her stomach, Liz thought when she entered the living-room, but her heart almost stopped beating when she saw Grant standing there facing the door.

Liz could not remember afterwards whether he had given her some indication, or whether she had taken the initiative, but she went into his arms as naturally as a pigeon to its nest, and buried her face against the jacket of his grey, lightweight suit. Their lips met somehow, and clung, and then she was easing herself a little away from his disturbing nearness.

'Why didn't someone tell me you were here?' she demanded breathlessly

'You would have been in the way.'

'Oh?'

'We had quite a few things to discuss.'

'Such as what, for instance?' she asked, tilting her head back and eyeing him suspiciously.

'Such as you and me, our wedding on Saturday afternoon at four o'clock, and the future,' he told her with a twisted smile, and her nerves knotted themselves into a tight ball.

'Grant——'

'Stacy has been very helpful, and we're being given these few minutes alone together so that I can give you this,' he brushed aside her fears and, dipping his hand into his jacket pocket, he brought out something which glittered brightly between his fingers.

It was a ruby, like a bright red drop of blood set in a circle of small diamonds, and her hand was shaking in his when he slipped it on to her finger. 'Oh, Grant,' she murmured unsteadily. 'How did you know it would fit so perfectly?'

'I came here this morning, and Stacy gave me one of your dress rings to take along with me.' Overcome with surprise, she could not think of anything to say until he gripped her fingers tightly and asked, 'Do you like it?'

'It's beautiful, but——'

'But?' he prompted when she halted abruptly to bite down hard on her quivering lip.

'You shouldn't have,' she managed in a choked voice, her eyes brimming with tears.

'I've never seen you cry before,' he announced with a mixture of concern and amusement.

'It's one of my many failings,' she laughed through her tears. 'When I'm happy I nearly always cry.'

His hands framed her face, and with a surprising display of tenderness he kissed away the tears that had escaped to roll down her cheeks.

'May we come in?' Stacy interrupted, knocking discreetly on the door.

'Yes, please do,' Grant announced gallantly as they

drew apart to see Stacy entering the living-room with Angus following close behind.

'I think this occasion calls for champagne, don't you?' said Angus, producing a bottle of the best.

'It certainly does,' Liz agreed, linking her arm through Grant's, and glancing up at him in an attempt to read his expression, but there was nothing there except amused tolerance.

The cork popped loudly from the neck of the bottle, and Angus proposed a grand toast. They drank their champagne and talked and laughed, and Liz could almost make herself believe that Grant was as happy as she if it were not for that distant look in his eyes which she glimpsed on several occasions. Was he thinking of Myra, and how different it had been when they had become engaged? Was he wishing that it was Myra who was wearing his ring on this occasion?

These thoughts hurt, and Liz found it extremely difficult making conversation during dinner that evening, but no one seemed to notice her lack of participation.

When Grant finally announced that it was time for him to leave it was natural for Liz to accompany him out to where he had parked his Jaguar. There were so many things she wanted to tell him, but the words simply would not come, and his preoccupation with his own thoughts made her feel worse.

'Will I see you tomorrow?' he asked, turning towards her in the darkness when they stood beside his car.

'Of course,' she replied with a forced brightness that sounded false to her own ears.

His hands were on her shoulders, his thumbs caressing the smooth skin below her collarbone, and sending delicious little tremors along her taut nerves. It had an almost therapeutic effect on her tense body, and she found herself relaxing, like a spring uncoiling slowly.

The evening had not been a roaring success, but the painful thoughts faded when his mouth found hers in the darkness, and she slid her arms inside his jacket, pressing closer to his hard length in an unconscious effort to ease away those stubborn little fears lurking in her mind.

'Grant,' she whispered eventually, straining a little away from him in an attempt to see his expression, but the moon had shifted behind the clouds, and his face was no more than a blur. 'If you want to change your mind about marrying me, I'll understand.'

'What makes you think I want to do that?'

'Nothing in particular.' She swallowed nervously. 'I'm simply giving you the opportunity to call the whole thing off if you have any doubts about it.'

His hands caressed her shoulders absently, his fingers slipping beneath the shoestring straps of her dress. 'I want to marry you, Liz, but I'm not totally convinced that I'm being fair to you.'

'You mean because of the way I feel about you?'

'Precisely.'

'You were honest with me, and honesty is all I shall ever ask of you,' she assured him, wondering if he knew how his feather-light caresses were affecting her pulse rate.

'I had a feeling you would say that, but——'

She silenced him with her fingers against his lips. 'I know what I want and, if you'll let me, I'll do my best to make you happy.'

'You're one of the most unselfish people I've ever

met, and I hope I never take advantage of you because of it,' he said when she had removed her fingers, then he was kissing her with a mastery that shut out everything except the fire his lips kindled. He caressed her with a sensual slowness, his hands warm through the thinness of her dress, and they lingered briefly against the thrusting swell of her breasts before he put her aside gently. 'Goodnight, Liz,' he murmured thickly, then he was getting into his car and driving away.

For the second time in less than two months Liz was packing. She had gone out to Grant's cottage the Friday morning, but that had been the last time she would see him until they met in church. The Saturday morning was hectic. There were so many last-minute things to pack before Angus transferred her belongings to High Ridges, and Liz was beginning to feel as if she had been caught unprepared in a bush fire.

Through it all she wondered, 'What is Grant doing? Is he as nervous as I am, or don't men suffer from pre-wedding nerves?'

'Is this the last?' Angus interrupted her thoughts when he entered her room and picked up the two suitcases she had placed beside the door. Perspiration glistened on his rugged face, and formed wide, damp patches on his shirt under the armpits, but his smile had not wavered once that morning.

'That's the lot,' Liz confirmed, her glance sweeping the room methodically.

'What about that?' Angus queried, gesturing with his head towards her vanity case on the bed.

'That will have to go with me.'

'You'd better hurry, Angus,' Stacy interrupted, rushing into Liz's room. 'Don't forget you still have to shower and change when you return from High Ridges.'

'There's plenty of time, darling,' he grinned at her. 'It's only one-thirty now.'

'That gives us a little more than two hours,' Stacy wailed, and she literally pushed Angus on his way.

A little more than two hours, Stacy's words echoed through Liz's mind when she found herself alone again. In a little more than two hours she would be Mrs Grant Battersby, and she was not quite sure whether she ought to feel nervous, or afraid. At the moment she felt neither; she felt extraordinarily calm, and there was no need to wonder why. She was marrying the man she had loved almost all her life, and if that little quiver at the pit of her stomach had to be analysed, then she would attribute it to excitement at the knowledge that her most impossible dream had come true.

Her glance travelled over the bright little room with its floral curtains. 'Tonight I'll be sleeping at Grant's cottage, in his bed, in his arms, and . . . oh, God,' she prayed silently, 'I don't ever want to let him down in any way.'

The hands of the clock on the bedside cupboard were reaching towards two o'clock when Liz grabbed her sponge bag and towel, and hurried along the passage to the bathroom. She could hear Rosalie crying, demanding her feed before Stacy took her along to the neighbour who had offered to take care of her while everyone else was at the church, and moments later everything was quiet except for the sound of water running into the bath.

Stacy came into Liz's room later that afternoon when she was doing her make-up, and her grave brown eyes met Liz's in the mirror. 'This may be the only moment I'll have to talk to you privately before the wedding.'

'Don't lecture me, Stacy,' Liz begged. 'Not today, please.'

'I don't want to lecture you, darling,' Stacy smiled shakily. 'I merely want you to know that, if you should need me, I'll always be here.'

'Oh, Stacy!' Liz blinked away her tears and, rising to her feet, she hugged her sister tightly. 'I knew I could count on you, and . . . thank you!'

Fifteen minutes later Angus was driving them to the church, and Grant's Jaguar was parked outside the grey stone building when they arrived. Liz felt really nervous for the first time that day. Her hands were shaking, and her insides were knotted so tightly that she doubted they would ever manage to unravel themselves again.

Grant was in the foyer, and her heart somersaulted in her breast at the sight of him. He looked exceedingly handsome in a dark grey suit and matching tie, and his limp was barely noticeable when he walked towards them. Their hands met, and her nervousness evaporated like mist before the sun on that warm April afternoon when his eyes smiled down into hers.

It was an unusual wedding with none of the usual ceremonies attached to it, but it was the most memorable day in Liz's entire life. They were married quietly, with Angus and Stacy as the only witnesses to the occasion, and two large tears rolled down Liz's cheeks when at last they stepped out into the sunshine. Grant pressed his handkerchief into her hands and, with an embarrassed laugh, she hastily repaired the damage before Angus and Stacy showered them unexpectedly with confetti.

'I have champagne waiting for us at the hotel,' Grant announced, brushing the remaining traces of confetti off his immaculate suit. 'We'll meet you there in the lounge.'

'We'll understand if you take a wee bit of time getting there,' Angus teased as he and Stacy got into their car, and then Grant's hand was beneath Liz's elbow to guide her towards his Jaguar.

Neither of them spoke when he drove away from the church, and neither did she question him when she realised that they were going in the opposite direction to the one Angus and Stacy had taken. A little distance out of town he turned off on to a quiet road, and parked the car in a shady spot used by travellers.

'I had to have you to myself for a few minutes,' he said, taking off her hat and flinging it on to the back seat, then she was in his arms and he was kissing her with a passionate intensity that made her senses whirl.

When at last he eased his mouth from hers to nuzzle her throat, she was breathless and flushed, and not quite capable of thinking straight.

'I needed that,' he groaned, and Liz admitted to herself silently that so had she.

They headed back to Pietersburg a few minutes later to join Angus and Stacy at the hotel for the champagne Grant had promised them, and Liz felt quite light-headed two hours later when she found herself alone once more with Grant, but he had yet another surprise in store for her. He had arranged for them to have dinner at a restaurant in town before going out to High Ridges and, when they faced each other across the small corner table with the candle flickering between them, Liz felt certain that everyone must have guessed

that they had been married only a few hours. She felt
flushed and happy, and she could not take her eyes off
Grant. He was so incredibly good-looking, and he was
her husband.

They lingered over their meal, talking about whatever came to mind, and Liz continued to be totally
oblivious of everyone else except Grant.

'It's been a long day,' he said much later when they
were having their coffee.

'I couldn't agree with you more.'

'Shall we go?'

Her eyes met his across the table, and her smile was
teasingly provocative. 'I thought you'd never suggest
it!'

She heard him draw a sharp breath, then a devilish
smile curved his mouth as he leaned towards her and
caught her fingers in his. 'You're a little witch,' he
said through his teeth. 'Let's go.'

Liz was amazed at herself for leading him on in that
extraordinary manner, but she still felt lightheaded as
a result of the amount of champagne she had con-
sumed, and it definitely made her feel quite daring.

CHAPTER FIVE

LIZ stared at the large bed with the headboard padded in brown leather, then she swung round towards the dressing-table to brush her corn-gold hair with unnecessary vigour. She was scared! Dammit, she was as scared as a cornered rabbit! And she looked it too, she decided when she stared at herself in the mirror. Her face was pale, her eyes wide and apprehensive and, underneath the lacy pink negligé which had been a gift from Stacy, her body quivered like a tautly strung violin.

She was Grant's wife, and the visible proof of his possession gleamed on the ring finger of her left hand. The plain gold wedding band with the unusual engagement ring felt heavy and unfamiliar; as unfamiliar as the knowledge that from now on she would be sharing his bed, and his life. Did every bride feel like this on her wedding night? she wondered frantically. Was it natural to feel nervy and edgy, and a little afraid of the physical side of loving?

The door opened unexpectedly, and she turned to see Grant standing there in a grey, patterned robe of expensive silk. She was conscious suddenly of several things at once; the anxious thudding of her heart, the transparency of her night attire, and an unmistakable flicker of desire in those steel-grey eyes when they slid over her with a slow sensuality that made her body feel heated with embarrassment. He closed the door behind him, almost as if he were shutting them off from the rest of the world, and the brush fell from her numb fingers to land with a thud at her feet. The sound jarred her nerves, but he caught her trembling hands in his before she could stoop to pick up the brush.

'Don't tell me you're nervous,' he mocked her.

This was not the time for pretence and, dragging her eyes from his hair-roughened chest above the V of his robe, she met his mocking glance and said unsteadily, 'I am nervous.'

'What was that provocative, come-hither attitude in aid of then?' he demanded with a derisive twist to his mouth that made her shrink inwardly.

'I'm not used to drinking so much champagne, and it made me feel more daring than usual.'

'And now you've got cold feet.'

The sneer in his voice hurt, and she dragged her hands free of his. 'I've never slept with a man before,' she explained defensively.

'Do you think I don't know that?' he murmured, his expression softening slightly.

'What if I disappoint you?' she voiced her fears at last.

He raised a hand and trailed a lazy, seductive path along the column of her throat down towards the plunging neckline of her negligé. She almost stopped breathing when his finger dipped into that enchanting valley between her breasts, but his hand trailed upwards again, and his fingers finally came to rest against that little pulse at the base of her throat which was fluttering so madly.

'You won't disappoint me, Liz,' he announced in a deep, throaty voice that was in itself a caress.

'How can you be so sure?'

His mouth curved in a sensuous smile. 'Perhaps I

know you a great deal better than you think.'

His fingers tugged at the satiny ribbon while he spoke, and her negligé parted to reveal an even flimsier garment beneath. Liz's heart was beating in her throat, almost choking off her breath, and she felt certain that she was blushing from her toes up to the roots of her hair when his hands slid down her arms in a single caress which resulted in her negligé lying in a heap at her feet.

'You're shy,' Grant accused with a soft laugh as he observed her heightened colour. 'I would never have believed it.'

'Do—Do you think you could put out the light?' she stammered in her confusion and embarrassment.

'If it will make you feel any better, then by all means.'

He moved away from her and flicked the switch beside the door. Blinded by the sudden darkness she stood there wishing that she could hide somewhere, but he was beside her in an instant, his warm mouth seeking and finding hers, and his hands sliding the straps of her nightdress off her shoulders so that it followed the path of her negligé.

Nothing, not even the darkness, could protect her now from the sensually arousing touch of his hands as they acquainted themselves with her untutored body. She trembled, hovering between painful shyness and sublime ecstasy as every nerve and sinew seemed to come alive to his touch, but when his thumbs moved in an erotic caress against the taut, rosy peaks of her breasts, she locked her arms about his neck and surrendered herself to the exquisite sensations he was arousing within her.

His hands slid down to her hips, drawing her closer

to his robed body, but he muttered impatiently the next instant, and drew a little away from her to tug at his belt. His robe parted, and she was pulled inside. For the first time in her life her naked body became acquainted with the hard, muscled flesh of a virile man, but her faint gasp went unnoticed as Grant buried his lips against the soft warmth of her throat before seeking her quivering mouth.

Liz was lost, and she found herself responding in an unfamiliar torrent of passion which seemed to burst forth inside her like a primitive being breaking the chains of its long captivity. She could no longer think coherently, only feel, and she had a curious sensation that she was floating before she felt the coolness of the bed beneath her and realised that he had lifted her on to it.

'Grant?' she groaned, a flicker of uncertainty invading this strange paradise as he shrugged himself out of his robe before joining her on the bed and drawing her once again into the curve of his body.

'Hm . . .?' he murmured absently, his sensual mouth exploring the curve of her breast, and the intimacy of his caress aroused a sweet stab of desire she had never known before.

'Oh, Grant, I love you!' the words spilled from her lips, then she surrendered herself completely to his passionate demands.

When Liz stirred and opened her eyes the following morning it took her several startled seconds to realise where she was. She was alone in Grant's bed, but she had spent most of the night in his arms, with his heavy thigh flung across her own and his arm about her waist as if he had been afraid she would slip away from him.

The memory of what had occurred between them still had the power to make her blush. There was not an inch of her body he had not acquainted himself with the night before. He had, she realised, been frighteningly thorough in breaking down her reserve, and she had responded to his intimate caresses until she had been aflame with desire and an aching need to be closer to him still. Never, not even by the wildest stretch of her imagination, could she have known what would follow. Her body had become an instrument of pleasure; his pleasure and her own, and together they had climbed the heights towards an exquisite release which had left her shattered and amazed at the intensity of the feelings she had not known she possessed.

Thinking of it now it filled her with awe and wonder, and a melting warmth invaded her body when she recalled his tender caresses in the aftermath of their passion. Her shyness temporarily forgotten, she had gone to sleep with her head on his shoulder, and the steady beat of his heart comfortingly beneath her ear.

Liz stretched and yawned, but one glance at the clock on the bedside cupboard made her leap out of bed. It was eight-thirty. She had slept much too late, and ... *hell*, she had nothing on! She snatched the sheet about her, but a second later she was laughing at herself. There was no one to witness her nakedness except the whitewashed walls and, dropping the sheet, she crossed the room and rummaged in one of her suitcases until she found her old cotton housecoat. She still had to unpack, but she could do that later, and she wrapped her housecoat about her as she went through to the bathroom across the passage from the bedroom.

A half hour later, bathed and dressed in beige slacks and an emerald green blouse, Liz invaded the kitchen, and prepared a belated breakfast. She was popping two slices of bread into the toaster when tanned, hair-roughened arms slipped about her waist, and she jumped with fright.

'Must you come in so silently and scare the living daylights out of me?' she rebuked him laughingly, turning in his arms and raising her face to his in a silent invitation which he did not ignore.

He kissed her lingeringly as if he were savouring the taste of her mouth, and when at last he raised his head she found herself confronted by a wicked gleam in his eyes.

'Did you have pleasant dreams?' he asked.

'I didn't dream at all,' she confessed. 'I slept as if someone had knocked me over the head with a sledge-hammer.'

'Was I that rough with you?'

The mockery in his eyes sent the blood surging into her cheeks, and she buried her face against his chest. 'Don't tease,' she begged.

'Your shyness fascinates me,' he laughed, prising her face out into the open. 'You've hidden it well behind your sharp-tongued exterior.'

'Well, now you know.'

'Yes, now I know.' Grant's mouth curved sensually, and his eyes lingered on her flushed cheeks and quivering mouth. 'I also made several other interesting discoveries about you.'

'The toast!' she protested, trying to escape from him when she heard the bread pop out of the toaster, but his arms merely tightened about her.

'It can wait,' he said, and his mouth descended to silence whatever protests she might still have wanted to make.

Her resistance fled, and she melted against him, yielding to the magic of his lips and hands while she tried to make herself believe that he loved her as much as she loved him.

The toast was cold when he eventually released her, and the omelettes had become a little leathery, but Grant did not complain, and Liz was too happy to care what she was eating.

'It's a lovely day,' said Grant when she poured his coffee. 'What about packing a picnic lunch and going for a long walk with me along the river. I must have plenty of excercise, you know.' He smiled at her wickedly. 'Doctor's orders.'

'You no longer need to walk with a stick, so a little bullying does help sometimes,' she laughed at him.

'I don't want to be bullied today,' he growled at her with mock-severity. 'What about that picnic I suggested?'

'I think it's a lovely idea,' she agreed enthusiastically.

It was a warm Sunday morning, and the tangy smell of the bush was all around them when they strolled along the river's edge up to where it widened into a small, sheltered lake. Their lunch was in the canvas bag which Grant had slung carelessly across one shoulder, and they were ravenously hungry when they flung themselves down on to the soft, wild grass beneath the willow and mimosa trees.

They ate their chicken sandwiches, nibbled at biscuits, and drank champagne out of tin mugs. It was crazy, but Liz loved every minute of it. Grant was again the man she had known all those years ago and, if it were at all possible, she fell in love with him all over again. He looked so tanned, so vital, so relaxed, and except for the premature greyness at his temples she could almost have flicked the calendar back six years. She wanted to touch him, but she was a little afraid to, so she rolled over on to her stomach and studied him where he lay beside her. His eyes were closed, and she allowed herself the pleasure of looking at his perfectly chiselled features, her eyes lingering for interminable seconds on his mouth. The desire to brush her lips against his was incredibly strong, but she was still slightly hesitant at the thought of indulging in such familiarities with this complex man she had married only the day before. He knew that she loved him, but she would have to take care not to smother him with her feelings.

Grant stirred and opened his eyes, and she looked away quickly, saying the first thing that came to mind.

'Did you know that when I was sixteen I thought you were the handsomest man on this earth?' Her tongue was running away with her, but it was nevertheless the truth.

'I don't doubt that you've changed your mind since then.'

'Oh, no,' she smiled down at him with teasing sincerity. 'I still think you're the handsomest man on this earth.'

Grant laughed out loud, his eyes crinkling at the corners, and his strong teeth flashing white against his tanned face.

The years in between seemed to roll away, and she said quietly, 'You should laugh more often.'

'I'm sure you'll keep me amused,' he mocked her.

'I shall do my best, sir.' He raised his hand to touch her cheek, and she caught it between her own to examine the raised scars. 'Grant . . . about your hand.'

He jerked his hand free, and sat up. 'We won't discuss it.'

'But you——'

'I said we won't discuss it!'

Liz sat up slowly, aware of his anger and displeasure in the way he picked up a twig and twisted it between his fingers. She observed his hands absently for a moment, then more intently, and her mouth tightened with determination. 'Don't be a coward, Grant.'

He turned on her, his eyes glacier-cold. 'What did you say?'

'I said, don't be a coward.'

His face became distorted with rage. 'My God, I——'

'Look!' She was up on her knees in front of him, her hands gripping his wrists, and his eyes followed the direction of her gaze. His right hand was gripping the twig almost as tightly as his left. 'If you haven't noticed the improvement, then I have,' she said angrily, 'and if you still don't want to discuss it after this, then you're a fool as well as a coward!'

She released his wrists and moved away from him, picking up the empty champagne bottle and mugs, and ramming them into the ruck-sack.

He sat there, almost as if he were in a daze, following every move she made with narrowed eyes. 'What are you doing?'

'Packing up,' she said stonily. 'We might as well return to the cottage.'

'Liz,' he growled, flinging the twig from him, and pulling her down towards him so that she fell heavily into his arms, 'you always were the most irritating thorn in my side. In the past I could always pluck you out, but now you're there permanently,' he said derisively, looking down into her wide, shadowed eyes.

'Do you expect me to sit back and do nothing while you stick your head in the sand like an ostrich, and stubbornly refuse to do anything about your career?'

'My career as a surgeon is finished,' he argued harshly, silencing her with a look when she wanted to interrupt. 'All right, so there's a slight improvement in my hand. Perhaps it wasn't as badly damaged as I first imagined, but what guarantee do I have that it will ever heal sufficiently for me to operate again?'

Liz stared up at him, at the way his crisp dark hair grew back from his broad forehead, the straight, high-bridged nose, and the strong, often sensuous mouth above the square, determined jaw. There was an un-mistakably deep anguish in his eyes, and she wanted to throw her arms around his neck in a rush of compassion, but she knew that this was the wrong moment to offer him sympathy.

'How often have you gone ahead with an operation without being able to give your patient the slightest guarantee that it would be a success?' Her eyes never wavered from his for a second as she thrust home her point. 'Do you want a written guarantee from someone before you'll let them make an attempt to help you?'

For a long time he said nothing, he simply looked at her intently, then he kissed her hard on the mouth, and set her aside. 'I think we've discussed this subject long enough. Let's go.'

The silences between them were strained. They both tried to make conversation on the way back to the cottage, but it just would not flow as it had done before. If only she could understand why someone with his determination should adopt such an attitude of defeat;

if only he would talk to her and explain!

That night, when he lay next to her without touching her, she knew that she could no longer tolerate the situation. She switched on the bedside light and sat up in bed.

'I'm sorry, Grant,' she said, staring with anguished eyes at the broad, muscled back which he had turned so resolutely towards her. 'I said all the wrong things again today.'

Grant remained stoically silent.

'Say something, for heaven's sake!' she pleaded. 'Accept my apology, or reject it, but please say *something*.'

'Acceptance doesn't come easily to me, and standing in the shadows as an instructor while someone else does the job is not something I relish,' he obliged her, pushing himself up against the pillows and lighting a cigarette. 'You've drawn my attention to the fact that there's some improvement in my hand, but I don't intend doing anything until I'm certain in my own mind that there's reason to get excited about it.'

Liz's mouth literally fell open in surprise. 'You mean you're not angry with me?'

'No, I'm not,' he smiled faintly, his eyes wandering to the thrust of her small breasts against the diaphanous garment she was wearing. 'I've been doing a lot of thinking, that's all.'

'About what I said?'

'That, *and* more.'

'Aren't you going to tell me about it?' she asked when he remained silent, but he shook his head and smiled that infuriating little smile that made her want to thump him hard on his chest with her fists. 'Why do you insist on shutting me out? Why can't you tell me what you're thinking, and what you feel?'

'I'll tell you what I'm thinking,' he said, putting out his half-smoked cigarette, and pulling her down beside him before she could prevent him. 'I think you're quite beautiful when you're angry, and I want you.'

'Stop that, and be serious.'

'I am serious,' he argued softly, brushing aside the flimsy strap of her nightdress and nibbling sensually at her throat and shoulder.

'Grant, we must talk,' she protested weakly, her mind resisting, but her body yielding to the velvety warmth of his hands against her skin as he helped her out of her nightdress.

'We'll talk tomorrow,' he growled in her ear, then his mouth shifted over hers, and she was lost as the fire of his passion washed over her.

The clean male smell of him, the exciting abrasiveness of his hair-roughened chest against her breasts, and his murmured words of passion all helped to seduce her until she cried out with the intensity of her aching need. No longer aware of what she was doing, she feverishly caressed his muscled back and slim hips. It was a joyous experience, touching him like this, exploring the smooth skin covering the hard flesh of his virile male body, and with a shudder he came over her, taking her with a fierceness which would have frightened her the night before, but which she now found intensely satisfying.

She went to sleep once again with her head on his shoulder, and her corn-gold hair spilling over his arm on to the pillow. She felt happy and momentarily secure, but deep down there was still that niggling fear that her good fortune might be no more than a fragile soap bubble.

The first two weeks of their marriage could not have been described as the most idyllic time Liz might have wished for, and the third week started off in much the same manner. Grant was often morose, lost in thoughts from which she was constantly excluded, and when she dared to question him he would slam out of the cottage and return some hours later, behaving as if nothing had happened. It frustrated Liz to the point of madness. She was never quite sure whether she could speak to him or not, and as a result she became tense and irritable, snapping at him quite often for no reason at all.

On the Tuesday evening of the third week, when he had helped her wash and pack away the dinner dishes, he turned to her and said quite unexpectedly, 'I'm returning to Johannesburg at the end of this week.'

Liz stared up at him in blank surprise, then she shivered as if he had emptied a tray of ice cubes down her back. 'And what about me?'

'You're coming with me, of course.'

'Oh?'

Grant glanced at her sharply, saw the paleness of her cheeks, and laughed shortly. 'Did you think I would leave you here?'

'It was the way you said it, I suppose,' she brushed aside his question in a controlled voice, but a spark of anger had been ignited within her. 'When did you come to this decision?'

'This morning,' he replied abruptly, taking his time lighting a cigarette, and leaning against the table as he blew the smoke towards the ceiling.

'May I know your plans, or shouldn't I ask?' she said when it seemed as if he was going to offer her no further explanation.

'You have a right to know.' He smiled derisively. 'You're my wife, aren't you?'

'I'm surprised you have remembered that when, just lately, you've been treating me like part of the furniture.'

He gestured angrily with the hand that held the cigarette. 'I've had quite a few heavy decisions to make.'

'I can imagine, but——'

'But?'

Liz chewed nervously on her bottom lip and shook her head. 'It doesn't matter.'

'You've never hesitated before to speak your mind,' he mocked her. 'Why start now?'

His mockery fanned that spark of anger into a flame, but somehow she managed to control her voice. 'I love you, Grant. I don't want to smother you, or embarrass you with my feelings, but I do wish you wouldn't shut me out so often.'

'Shut you out?'

'Yes,' she said, her hands clutching the cupboard behind her so that he would not see them shaking. 'From your thoughts, your hopes, and perhaps also your fears.'

'For heaven's sake, Liz!' he exploded savagely. 'Do you expect me to run to you with every little thought that crosses my mind?'

'No, of course not,' she argued. 'But you could share some of them with me—the important ones, at least.'

'But what the hell do you think I'm doing now?'

'You could have let me in on it while you were still considering this move,' she accused coldly.

'For God's sake!' he shouted, raising himself to his full height and raking her from head to foot with narrowed, furious eyes. 'Don't tell me I've got myself a nagging woman!'

The use of the word 'woman' instead of 'wife' triggered off her anger to the extent that she seemed to see his face through a red film of fury. 'Damn you, Grant! I don't just want to be the woman you take to bed with you at night. I want to be your wife in every sense of the word. I want to share the ups as well as the downs, the smooth as well as the rough, and I have every right to expect it.'

A chilling silence followed her outburst, then he asked in an ominously quiet voice, 'Have you finished?'

'Yes,' she whispered hoarsely.

'Then get this straight!' He put his face so close to hers that she could see the pores in his skin. 'When I asked you to marry me I told you quite clearly what I had to offer you, and you accepted my proposal on those terms. If you're not happy with our marriage as it is, then you can damn well *go* for all I care!'

He stormed out into the night, slamming the door so hard behind him that her ears ached with the sound of it, but the ache in her ears was nothing compared to the stabbing chill of his parting words. It was true, of course. She had accepted his proposal for what it was worth, and now it must seem to him that she was rebelling against it. If she did not like it, then she could go, he had said, but was that truly how he felt, or had he simply lashed out in anger.

Liz began to shake, but the tears would not come. They simply lodged in her throat until, gasping for breath, she lowered herself into a chair. She regained her control with difficulty, but that did not stop her mind from torturing her. What if he had been serious? The station-wagon stood parked outside, and all she had to do was load her things into it, and leave. Was that what Grant wanted? No . . . yes . . . *no*! Oh, God, she didn't know!

She picked up her sewing basket and sewed the buttons on to his shirt, but every few minutes she found herself glancing at the clock against the wall. He had been gone an hour. Where was he? What was he doing out there in the dark?

She switched on the kettle and made herself a cup of instant coffee, but she did so automatically while her mind flitted about outside, thinking of all the things that could possibly happen to Grant on such a dark night in the veld. She tortured herself with frightening visions until it felt as if she would go mad. She tried not to think while she curled her cold fingers around the mug and drank her coffee, but her mind refused to be stilled.

She eventually put away her sewing basket and glanced at the clock. Two hours! Grant had been gone two hours! It was late, and she was tired, but she knew that she would never sleep until she knew that he had returned safely.

Liz tried to ease away her tension and her fears in a hot, scented bath, but it was the sound of quick, heavy footsteps in the cottage that finally succeeded in chasing away some of her frightened thoughts. She stepped out of the bath, and was reaching for her towel when the bathroom door swung open.

Grant stood there, his hair awry, and his breathing a little uneven as she clasped the towel to her wet body and stared up at him with wide, anxious eyes. He looked pale beneath his tan, but she saw the muscles in his jaw relax, and she did not miss that flicker of relief in his eyes.

Without a word he stepped into the bathroom and closed the door behind him. The large towel was removed from her nerveless fingers, and very gently, as if she were a child, he rubbed her dry, then he took her cotton robe off the hook behind the door and held it for her to slip her arms into it.

'I was afraid for a moment that you might have gone,' he said, his eyes on her hands as she fastened the buttons down the front of her robe.

'I made you angry,' she said in a voice that was much steadier than her insides and, taking off her shower cap, she let her thick golden hair tumble down on to her slim shoulders. 'I hoped that was the reason for the things you said.'

A muscle jerked in his cheek, their eyes met, and then she was in his arms. They held each other tightly without speaking. What else was there to say except '*I love you*', but the words lodged in her aching throat, and she knew that Grant would never say them. He wanted her, he might even need her at times, but he would never love her.

'I'm glad you came this morning,' said Stacy when Liz dropped in for a cup of tea and a chat. From the drawer in the hall table she took out an airmail envelope and handed it to Liz. 'It's a letter from Pamela addressed to you.'

'Thanks,' Liz murmured absently, slipping the letter into her handbag.

'Aren't you going to read it?'

'I'll read it later,' said Liz, following her sister into the kitchen, and seating herself at the kitchen table while Stacy made a pot of tea and complained about Rosalie's fretfulness during the night. Liz drank her tea, and listened in silence, and they had discussed various subjects before she managed to voice the reason for her visit. 'Grant and I are going to Johannesburg on Friday.'

Stacy looked shocked, but she recovered swiftly to ask, 'Permanently, or for a visit?'

'Permanently.' Liz put down her cup and fiddled nervously with the teaspoon in her saucer. 'Grant wants to see a colleague of his who he thinks might be able to help him regain full use of his hand.'

'Do you think there's a possibility of that ever happening?'

'I'm confident that he'll operate again,' Liz replied without hesitation, but Stacy remained a little sceptical.

'Can you imagine what it will do to him if he's built up his hopes and finally discovers that the initial diagnosis was correct?'

Liz shrank inwardly from the implication in those words. 'I don't want to think about that.'

'You'll *have* to think about it, Liz,' Stacy persisted sensibly. 'You'll be there to witness his success, or his failure and, if it's the latter, you'll have to deal with it, and teach him how to live with it.'

Liz digested this slowly, realising that she could not turn her back for ever on something which might well happen. 'I can only help him if he'll let me.'

'What do you mean, *if* he'll let you?'

'Grant can be very stubborn if he wishes.'

'Hm ... I know what you mean,' Stacy muttered, and there was a hint of understanding in the smile she directed at Liz.

'To get back to the actual reason why I'm here,' Liz changed the subject. 'I want to leave the station-wagon here with you. Grant says it's far too cumbersome for me to travel in, and he's thinking of buying me a smaller car.' Her questioning gaze met Stacy's. 'Do you think Angus might be able to sell it for me?'

'I'm sure of it,' Stacy replied confidently. 'What do you want me to do with the money?'

'Keep it somewhere safe. Who knows,' Liz smiled wanly, 'I might need it some day.'

Stacy frowned. 'That's an odd thing to say, considering that you're married to a man as wealthy as Grant.'

'There are such things as rainy days, you know,' Liz reminded her, unable to explain her cautious approach into the future.

'You're not hiding something from me, are you?'

'I must go,' Liz prevaricated. 'I have a shopping list the length of my arm, and there's plenty to do before we leave on Friday.'

Liz felt deeply disturbed when she left Stacy's home a few minutes later. Why she should have this gnawing uncertainty about her future with Grant she could not say. She wished she could explain it to herself, but no answer seemed to be forthcoming.

CHAPTER SIX

IT was not until the afternoon following her visit to Stacy that Liz read Pamela's letter. She had been searching in her handbag for a pen when she found the letter and, feeling guilty, she slit it open with her thumb and drew out the single sheet of paper.

'Dear Liz,' Pamela's familiar handwriting scrawled across the paper, 'Stacy wrote and told me of your marriage to Grant. You could have written yourself, but I presume you were too busy. Who would have thought that my freckle-faced little sister would end up marrying the guy next door, and what a guy too!'

A smile plucked at the corners of Liz's wide mouth and, making herself comfortable on the bed, she read further. 'Congratulations, Liz, but take a word of advice from me before you celebrate your achievement in landing this particular fish. Watch out for Myra; she's like poison ivy, and she seldom lets go once she's hooked her claws into someone. A friend of mine in the fashion business ran across Myra in Paris a week ago. Her elderly sugar-daddy got wise to her, and she's at a loose end.'

Liz went cold as if someone had poured iced water into her veins, and she stared blankly out of the bedroom window for several seconds before she had the courage to read further.

'Don't be surprised, little sister, if Myra turns up like the proverbial bad penny, and my guess is she'll make a play for Grant. She had him once, and she has enough gall to think she could have him again. She fights dirty, Liz, and if you want to hold on to Grant then I suggest you do the same. Good luck, and God bless. Pamela.'

Liz's hands shook so much that the letter fell from her fingers on to her lap, and slid down to the floor. She felt too sick inside to move at first, but she was galvanised into feverish action when she heard Grant returning from his meeting with Sam Muller. She stooped to pick up Pamela's letter, and tore it into tiny shreds along with the envelope. It was as if she was attempting to tear up the threat of Myra's existence, and what she could do to their marriage, but Liz did not quite succeed in stilling that gnawing fear within her heart.

She dropped the pieces of paper into the bin beside the dressing-table mere seconds before Grant walked into the room, but she was not quite so successful in hiding the fact that something had upset her.

'What's the matter?' Grant demanded, his critical glance taking in her pale cheeks and trembling hands.

Whatever the cost he must never find out about Pamela's letter, nor its contents, and for the first time in her life she lied to him. 'I'm a little tired, I think.'

'Are you sure that's all it is?'

She avoided the close scrutiny of his eyes, and tried to smile. 'It's nothing serious.'

Not yet, she could have added, but she didn't, and Grant gestured her on to the bed. 'Put your feet up for a while, and I'll bring you a cup of tea.'

Liz felt a fraud lying there on the bed while she allowed Grant to pamper her with a cup of tea and concern. She wanted to scream the truth at him, but

she did not dare, so she acted out this disgusting charade
to the bitter end.

'At the rate you've been packing we could leave
within the hour instead of in the morning,' said Grant
eventually when he took the empty cup from her and
placed it on the bedside cupboard.

'I don't like leaving things to the last minute,' she
explained. 'That's when one is inclined to leave
something behind.'

'Don't forget to pack yourself, will you? I wouldn't
want to arrive in Johannesburg and find you're not in
any of the suitcases.'

'Silly!' she laughed, aiming a playful blow at his
strong jaw.

'It made you laugh, didn't it?'

Their eyes met and her laughter faded, leaving only
the terrible feeling that what she had was only tempor-
ary and, in one fluid movement, she sat up and threw
her arms about his neck.

'Oh, Grant!' she whispered brokenly against his
shoulder. 'Hold me tight, I'm so afraid.'

His arms were hard and comforting about her, and she
could feel his throat vibrating with soft laughter against
her lips. 'I'm the one who should be afraid, not you.'

Liz did not answer him, but simply clung to him in
a desperate effort to find some reassurance in the hard
warmth of his body against her own. How could she
tell him of her fears? How could she explain that gnawing suspicion that their time together was limited, and
how could she tell him of the uncertainty with which
she viewed the future now that she knew of the possibility that Myra might be returning to South Africa,
to her old hunting grounds, and to Grant in particular?
No! She would prefer him to think she was simply

afraid for him, and she decided to leave it at that.

Grant's home was a two-storied mansion set among trees, shrubs, and spacious lawns, and Liz felt as though she had arrived at a five-star hotel when white-coated servants appeared as if from nowhere to unload the car as well as the trailer Grant had attached to it.

The house was imposing on the inside as well as the outside, but it did not quite match up to Liz's idea of what a home ought to be. The furnishings were modern in the extreme in expensive glass and chrome, and the chairs in the living-room looked very much like elephant-sized bean-bags of the variety Liz used to play with as a child. There were mirrors everywhere, making the rooms appear larger than they already were, and ankle-deep shaggy carpets covered the floors. Ultra-modern paintings adorned the walls in every room, their colours bright, their symmetry precise, but none of them made sense. Grant took her on an inspection tour of the house, and Liz felt as though she were turning the pages of a glossy magazine which depicted only the very latest in furnishings. It was all very beautiful, and very impressive, but it lacked that homely, lived-in feeling.

'How on earth did you manage to live all on your own in a house this size?'

Ill-chosen words! She realised this the moment she caught that look in Grant's eyes. He had lived here with Myra, and Liz had been foolish enough not to realise it from the moment she had entered the house. Myra's stamp was all over the place, and the most glaring clue had been all those strategically placed mirrors. Myra was beautiful, and she thrived on the admiration of men almost as much as she enjoyed admiring herself. In this particular showcase there could have been no possibility of missing herself, for wherever one turned there was a mirror to catch a pose, gesture, or that look of admiration in a man's eyes even if he should be standing behind one.

There was, however, no admiration in Grant's eyes when they met hers in the mirror across the room, only cold disdain, and his very silence gave Liz the answer to her question. A little shiver coursed its way up her spine, and she wondered how she was going to live with him in this house which must hold so many memories of his long affair with the beautiful Myra Cavendish.

They were in the main bedroom, and Liz looked about her warily. One entire wall was mirrored, and so also the ceiling, and the adjoining bathroom was a mirrored fantasy with a sunken, heart-shaped bath which had been tiled in mosaic. There was something conceitedly feminine in what Liz saw, and she knew at once that this had been Myra's bedroom. Grant, she supposed, had shared it with Myra and, oh God! . . . she had to get out of it!

'I thought we could use the suite across the passage,' said Grant as if he had guessed her repulsive thoughts. 'It's smaller, it doesn't get as much sun, but it's less ostentatious.'

Relief washed over her almost like a belated blessing when he guided her into the suite he had mentioned. He was right, and there was nothing ostentatious about this room except perhaps the view from the window down on to the marble, oval-shaped pool, and tennis courts. There were no unnecessary mirrors, no glass and chrome, and no shaggy carpets. The colours were predominantly blue and white, and the furniture had been made of solid, sturdy wood. The adjoining bathroom was blessedly ordinary with white, tiled walls, and for the first time Liz felt genuine pleasure at what she saw.

'Yes, I like it,' she announced, smiling shakily up at Grant.

'I thought you would,' he said curtly. 'I'll have our bags brought up, and the rest of your things could go into that small lounge downstairs. You may refurnish it if you wish, and use it as a study to work in.'

'Thank you, Grant, and . . .' She caught at the sleeve of his jacket when he would have turned away. 'Don't be long.'

'You don't like this house, do you?' he mocked her.

She was glad he had called it a house, and not a home, for the nearest thing to *home* was this suite, and looking up into his eyes, she said carefully, 'Not very much.'

'We'll find ourselves something else in time.' He caught her chin between his fingers and kissed her briefly. 'I won't be long.'

While Grant was out Liz made use of the bathroom and freshened herself up after their long journey from Pietersburg. They had taken their time, stopping for lunch along the way, but Liz felt dry and in need of the tea Grant had ordered soon after their arrival.

He was waiting for her when she emerged from the bathroom. Their suitcases had been placed in a neat row at the foot of the bed, but the unpacking could wait until after they had had their tea. She linked her arm through Grant's when they went downstairs, and the mirrors reflected the images of a tall, dark, magnificently proportioned man, and a fair, slim girl whose head barely reached his shoulder. Liz could not help seeing herself in those hateful mirrors even though her gaze was directed at Grant. He looked as bronzed and fit as she had always remembered him. He no longer limped, and his long, lithe strides had been shortened to match hers. It was still difficult to believe that this man was her husband, and when at last she looked at her own image in the mirrors she found it equally difficult to understand why he had married her. She was plain in comparison with women such as Myra Cavendish, and her slim, straight figure was certainly not of the variety which would drive men wild with desire. Liz was so busy criticising herself that she missed entirely her two most outstanding features; her soft, generous mouth with the passionate curve to the upper lip, and her large brown eyes which might have been dipped in gold. Her eyes, if she but knew it, were the mirrors of her soul, and Grant, if he but cared to look, would have found there what most men spend their lives searching for.

Tea was served to them in the living-room, and Liz felt her facial muscles tighten while she poured. Myra's stamp was here as well, and the tea-cups were of modern pottery instead of conventional china. The desire was strong to fling the cups at the offending mirror against the opposite wall, but Liz controlled herself sufficiently to hide her irritation from Grant.

'I think I should start unpacking,' she said when they had had their tea and the conversation dwindled, but Grant took her hand and drew her out into the garden.

'It's all being taken care of,' he explained.

Liz felt odd. For the first time in her life someone else, other than herself, would be handling her clothes, and she could not quite decide whether she liked it or not, but she chose at that moment not to make an issue of it.

The enormous garden was an autumn serenade of green, gold, and vermilion, and the cool breeze scattered the fallen leaves into a colourful carpet beneath their feet. A thick strand of hair blew across her face, and when her attempts to brush it away were unsuccessful she removed the scarf from about her throat, intending to use it as a ribbon of sorts.

'Leave it,' Grant ordered at once, taking the scarf from her hands and pushing it into his jacket pocket. 'I prefer to see your hair blowing free like that.'

'But it's so untidy,' she protested.

'When you tie it back into a ponytail you become "Liz the horror".' His hands caressed her cheeks and her throat before becoming entangled in her hair. 'When you leave it free like this I don't somehow have the feeling that I've robbed the cradle.'

'Poor dear,' she teased, trying to ignore the way his nearness stirred her senses. 'Do I make you feel ancient?'

'It's not that I feel particularly ancient,' he smiled, sliding his hands down her back and drawing her closer until the muscled hardness of his hips and thighs were against her own. 'The problem is that you're so young,' he dropped the proverbial ball back into her court.

'If you'd said that to me six years ago then I could have understood it,' she said against his descending mouth. 'I was so young then you barely noticed me.'

'Oh, I noticed you all right,' he laughed deep in his throat. 'You foiled every single attempt I made to get Pamela to myself, and I could have wrung your little neck at times,' he informed her in between tantalising kisses.

'You always looked as if you were ready to conquer the world, let alone Pamela, and I had to do something to keep your male ego intact.'

He raised his head and smiled derisively down into her eyes. 'You imagined I would fail with Pamela?'

'I didn't imagine it, I knew it,' she stated emphatically. 'Pamela was always a flirt, but she had rigid principles with regard to sex.'

'What makes you think she wouldn't have discarded her principles for me?'

'We three Holden girls are as different as cheese, chalk, and *mealie pap*, but we do have one thing in common.' Liz leaned back in the circle of his arms and raised her grave face to his. 'We have to love a man before we'll allow him to take liberties of such an intimate nature, and then it must occur within the bounds of marriage.'

'Marriage before sex is considered old-fashioned,' he mocked her.

'If that's your opinion then why didn't you attempt to lure me into your bed before we were married?'

He released her so abruptly she would have fallen had she not been holding on to his shoulders, but she let go the minute she steadied herself.

'I'd lost my appetite for that kind of relationship with a woman,' he explained harshly, thrusting his hands into his pockets and turning from her. 'I wanted a marriage, something stable and solid, and I knew that with you I could have the kind of life I wanted.'

A joyous warmth invaded her heart and brought a light of tenderness to her eyes. 'I think that's the nicest compliment you've ever paid me.'

His lips twitched. 'It wasn't intended as a compliment.'

'You don't mind if I take it as one, do you?'

'Please yourself.'

She *would* please herself, she decided, slipping her arm through his when they walked back to the house. It was gratifying to know that he had considered her capable of giving him the stability he had needed in marriage, and it was something she would cling to if ever she had doubts about their future.

Liz felt lost somehow with nothing to do. Their suitcases had been unpacked and neatly stashed away in one of the built-in cupboards, and Grant had told her quite bluntly that she would not be needed in the kitchen. What, she wondered, had Myra done with herself all day? But then, Liz supposed, Myra's modelling career must have kept her extremely busy, and this house must have been simply a place to sleep in, or a spacious venue in which to entertain her friends and Grant's.

Damn Myra Cavendish! Liz did not want to think of her, but she could not help herself. She felt her presence everywhere, from the grotesque-looking Buddha in the hall to the lingering fragrance of her heady, expensive perfume in the room across the passage. Oh, why did Grant have to bring her here to this house of mirrors with its memories of another woman?

Dinner that evening was a five-course meal which made Liz feel ashamed of her own elaborate efforts in the kitchen—prawn cocktails, celery soup, fish soufflé, tender veal with the greenest peas she had ever seen, and small baked potatoes. To round off the meal they had date sponge and butterscotch sauce, with cheese and biscuits to follow.

Their coffee was served in the living-room, and Liz felt mentally winded by the time they went upstairs to their room. It was like living in a different world; a starchy world which seemed light years away from those cosy evenings around the kitchen table with the dishes piled high in the sink, and a mug of coffee in their hands. She felt sad, too, as if she had lost something which might never be returned to her, and she swallowed convulsively at the lump which had risen in her throat.

Grant showered while Liz soaked in the bath, and he was lying in bed smoking a cigarette when she finally came out of the bathroom. He smoked less these days, and it was something for which she was grateful, but at that moment she was more concerned with her senses being stirred at the sight of his wide, bare chest where the dark, rough hair curled tightly against his bronzed skin. The muscles were taut across his flat stomach, and she had been married to him long enough to know that beneath the sheet he was narrow-hipped and long-limbed with muscled thighs and calves. Along the outer side of his right thigh there was a neat scar where they had had to make an incision to reset the shattered bone, and Liz prayed with all her heart that the healing process would be repeated in his sluggish hand.

She turned away from the distraction of his muscled torso and brushed her hair vigorously until it shone. She could feel him observing her as she had observed him, and she nervously said the first thing that came to mind.

'I'm obviously going to have plenty of time to write.'

'You may please yourself,' he replied in a bored-sounding voice. 'You could write your little stories, or simply be a lady of leisure.'

'The latter doesn't appeal to me very much,' she laughed, putting down her brush and walking round to her side of the bed. 'When do you have to see this colleague of yours?' she changed the subject.

'Monday morning first thing.'

'Will I be allowed to come with you?' she asked, slipping out of her robe and getting into bed beside him.

'Does it look as though I'm going to need someone to hold my hand?' he mocked her.

'A little moral support has never hurt anyone,' she retorted stiffly. 'I'd like to go with you, if I may.'

He shrugged and put out his cigarette. 'Please yourself.'

There it was again for the third time that day. *Please yourself*. The first time she had been too thrilled to bother about it, the second time she could still accept it, but the third time was just too much.

'Stop saying that!' she snapped angrily. 'It's not myself I want to please, but you!'

A heavy silence settled between them, then Grant turned to her and said something totally unexpected. 'I don't deserve a wife like you.'

'You deserve much better, but I'm doing my best to live up to your expectations,' she managed when the tension eased within her.

'I think I'd like you to go with me.' He rolled towards her and his hand slid in a sensual caress up along her smooth thigh. 'It's one way of introducing you to someone who's not just a colleague but a friend.'

'Now you're making me nervous,' she muttered, finding it difficult to think straight, and wondering if he was aware of what his caressing hand was doing to her. 'What if your friends don't like me?'

Grant was leaning over her, forcing her down on to the pillows, and the heat of his body against her own was awakening that familiar longing which she found so impossible to control.

'My friends are city people,' he said, tracing the outline of her lips with a sensual finger. 'Your fresh country looks will appeal to them.'

'Why do I have that horrible feeling that you're making fun of me?'

'What I've said is the truth. They'll love your hair,' he assured her, and tugged at it playfully. 'It's like ripe corn, and they'll adore your freckles—all sixteen of them.'

'I no longer have any freckles.'

'When your face is scrubbed clean as it is now, then they're clearly visible. There's one there . . . and there . . . and there . . .' His kisses on her small, straight nose punctuated his words.

'Stop it!' she protested, warding off his lips.

'You smell nice,' he murmured, his hand in her hair tipping her head back to expose her throat for the fiery exploration of his lips. 'Hm . . . girlish and sweet.'

'Grant . . .' she sighed, melting helplessly against him.

'Sweet enough to eat,' he growled, then his mouth shifted over hers to satisfy her growing need . . . and his.

Alan Bishop's consulting-rooms were situated in the new medical centre, and when Grant and Liz arrived there early on the Monday morning they were ushered in to see him at once.

Grant's colleague was a stockily-built man with nondescript brown hair, smiling features, and shrewd brown eyes, and he stepped out from behind his desk the moment they entered the room to take Grant's hand in a welcoming gesture.

'It's good to see you again, Grant.'

'Alan, I'd like you to meet my wife.' Brown eyes swivelled in Liz's direction as Grant made the necessary introduction, and if Alan Bishop was surprised, then he hid the fact extremely well. 'Liz, this is Alan Bishop.'

'It's a pleasure to meet you, Liz.' His hand engulfed hers, and she decided that he had a nice smile as well as a pleasing voice, then he released her hand and turned once more to Grant. 'You're looking great.'

'I feel good,' Grant confessed.

Alan's smile deepened with mischief when he glanced at Liz. 'You must have been just the right tonic he needed.'

'In small dosages I'm potent, but in large quantities I'm like dynamite,' she replied with a sweet humour that made Alan and Grant burst out laughing.

'I can see why you married her,' Alan remarked at length to Grant, then he gestured him into a chair. 'Let's take a look at your hand.'

Alan Bishop's examination was thorough, his questions brief and to the point, and it was clear to Liz that he was not the type to leave anything to chance.

She felt Grant's tension as if it were her own, and after a few minutes which had seemed like an eternity, Grant's voice sliced through the silence in the room.

'Well?' he demanded.

'It's difficult to say,' Alan frowned, his lower lip jutting out as if he were deep in thought. 'There's a definite improvement, but I would like to have your hand X-rayed before I give you my final opinion.'

'Then let's get on with it,' Grant replied with that familiar thread of impatience in his deep voice.

Alan stretched out a hand towards the telephone and lifted the receiver. 'I'll let the radiology department know you're on your way, and I'll bring the results to your home this evening.'

The consultation with Alan Bishop had taken no more than a half hour, but at the radiology department, three floors up, it was quite a different matter. They had no option but to wait an hour before they could fit Grant into their busy schedule, then a power failure delayed them another forty-five minutes before they could proceed with the X-rays. It was almost midday before they finally emerged from the building, and by that time Grant was in a fury which was hot enough to set fire to the medical centre.

'How many of your patients have been kept waiting because of circumstances beyond your control?' she demanded bluntly when everything else failed to calm him down, and she thought for a moment he was going to strike her, but instead the tension and anger drained slowly from his face to be replaced by a wry smile.

'You have a point there,' he admitted, placing his arm about her shoulders as they crossed the car park to where he had left the Jaguar, and Liz sighed inwardly with relief when he finally turned to her in the car and said: 'What about lunch somewhere before we go home?'

'That would be nice,' she agreed and, leaning towards him, she kissed him impulsively on the lips.

'What was that for?' he grinned.

'Just to let you know that I think you're one of the nicest men I know,' she smiled at him with mischief dancing in her eyes, then she kissed him once again, and settled back comfortably in her seat.

'Crazy woman,' he growled, but there was a gleam of laughter in his eyes when he started the car and set it in motion.

They went to a small restaurant in Hillbrow with a faintly continental atmosphere about it. Basket lanterns dangled above tables covered with checkered cloths, and soft, recorded music was relayed over hidden speakers. The place was not overcrowded, and Liz liked it at once.

'You specialise in neuro-surgery, don't you?' she questioned Grant conversationally when he had placed their order.

'I *did*, yes,' he replied, stressing the past tense, but she ignored it.

'That's intricate work, isn't it?'

'It is.'

'Relax, Grant,' she urged softly when she recognised the signs of strain and tension on his face. 'You have nothing to worry about.'

He smiled twistedly. 'I wish I had your confidence, Liz, but this is so very important to me.'

'I know.'

'What if——'

'Don't say it! Don't even think it!'

'The positive approach, is that it?' he questioned her with a hint of humour in his glance, and she nodded.

'Exactly.'

'In that case let's be premature and order a bottle of champagne.'

'I think that's a brilliant idea,' she laughed softly, and he raised his hand to summon the wine steward.

They took almost two hours over lunch, but Liz was

reluctant to leave the restaurant with its cosy, relaxed atmosphere. The afternoon lay ahead of them, the long hours of waiting, wondering and worrying before they could expect Alan Bishop to arrive with the results of the X-rays. For Liz it would be difficult, but for Grant it was going to be intolerable. She had to think of something; of some way to keep him occupied, but her mind remained an awful blank in that direction.

Grant paid the bill and Liz sensed that he was thinking similar thoughts when they walked back to the car in silence. How was he going to pass the time until Alan called that evening?

He held open the door for her on the passenger side and closed it the moment she was in, then he walked round to the driver's side. A child skipped by with a toy elephant under the arm, and it was as if someone had flicked a switch in Liz's mind.

'Let's go to the zoo,' she suggested, turning excitedly towards Grant.

'The zoo?' he queried with a blank, almost startled look on his face.

'I'm told that's where they keep all the animals,' she mocked him lightly.

'So I've heard.'

She leaned towards him anxiously. 'Will you take me?'

'If you really want to go,' he sighed resignedly.

'You're so kind,' she teased.

That mocking, faintly humorous note in her voice did not escape him, and he eyed her with mock severity when he had inserted the key in the car's ignition. 'Remind me to buy you an ice-cream when we're there, but I draw the line at a stick of candy-floss.'

'Spoilsport!' she accused laughingly, wrinkling her

nose at him, but deep down she felt relieved and somewhat triumphant.

It was a surprisingly warm afternoon, considering that winter was on the doorstep, and as it was a Monday there were not as many people wandering about in the cleverly constructed zoological gardens where the animals appeared to be roaming as freely as the visitors.

Liz dragged Grant from one end of the zoo to the other, lingering for a while beside each different species to discuss it before they went on to the next. She was determined not to give him a moment in which to brood about whatever news Alan would have for them that evening, but when they approached the giraffes Grant was beginning to show definite signs of becoming bored and restless.

'Did you know that to the early Romans the giraffe was considered to be a mythical creature with a leopard for its father and a camel for its mother?' Liz remarked, determined not to give up.

'No, I didn't know, and I'm duly impressed,' he announced, but his expression told her something quite the opposite.

'The name "giraffe" comes from the Arab *zirafah* which has a twofold meaning; "a creature of grace", and "one who walks swiftly".'

'Talking about walking,' Grant interrupted caustically, 'I don't think I can walk another step.'

'I think I read somewhere that the first giraffe to reach Europe had been imported by Julius Caesar, and he exhibited it in Rome in 46 B.C., or somewhere around there.'

'Liz——'

'I believe a giraffe weighs——'

'*Liz!*'

His hand gripped her arm, and her smile was sweetly innocent when he swung her round to face him. 'Yes, darling?' she asked softly.

'You've been an energetic and informative guide all afternoon, and you've succeeded in your objective, but I think we should leave before we're caught in the five o'clock traffic.'

The realisation that he had guessed her reasons for bringing him there filled her with dismay, and faint embarrassment. 'I couldn't let you sit around and worry yourself silly all afternoon,' she explained lamely. 'I'm sorry.'

With his fingers beneath her chin he tipped up her face, forcing her to meet his eyes, and what she saw there made her pulse rate quicken. Everything else faded into insignificance except for that tender light in the eyes of the man she loved, and she wished she could capture this moment to preserve it for the rest of her life.

His glance shifted beyond her and back again. 'If that warden over there wasn't watching us, I'd kiss you.'

'Funny,' she whispered impishly without taking her eyes off him, 'but I don't see a warden anywhere.'

Grant's laughter was a rumbling sound deep down in his throat, and lowering his dark head he kissed her on her quivering mouth until her lips tingled. Too soon he eased himself away from her, and there was a coolness in his voice when he gripped her arm and said abruptly, 'Come on, let's go.'

CHAPTER SEVEN

ALAN Bishop arrived at the house shortly after seven that evening, and he was shown directly into the living-room. Liz felt incredibly tense while Grant poured out a drink for Alan and the usual platitudes were exchanged, but she was not the only one who was feeling the strain. Grant smiled with his lips, but his eyes had that haunted look which she had seen so often during those days before their marriage.

'Let's get to the point,' Grant said eventually in a cool, clipped voice. 'What are my chances?'

Alan swirled the ice cubes around in his drink and swallowed down a mouthful of whisky before he spoke. 'After a small operation and plenty of therapy, I think there's a strong possibility that you'll be operating again before the end of this year.'

'Only a possibility?' Grant demanded harshly, his mouth drawn into a tight line.

'I said a *strong* possibility,' Alan emphasised, lifting the flap of the large brown envelope he had brought with him, and taking out the X-rays. 'Take a look at these and judge for yourself.'

Grant took the X-rays from him and walked towards the light which hung like a large soap bubble against the opposite wall, and Alan put down his drink to follow him there. Liz sat very still and erect in her chair while they studied the X-rays and discussed them in medical terms which made no sense to her at all. The news had been disappointing in one way and another. She had expected something more definite, but miracles and instant cures, she supposed, were something which occurred only in books.

'When can you do the operation?' Grant was questioning Alan when they returned to their chairs.

'I'll make arrangements for you to be admitted to hospital tomorrow afternoon, and I'll do it first thing Wednesday morning.'

'Good,' Grant muttered, topping up their whisky glasses.

'Here's to you,' said Alan, raising his glass in a salute to Grant, and he smiled again that warm friendly smile Liz had seen that morning.

She found herself relaxing, and her confidence returned swiftly. Perhaps it had something to do with Alan's easy approach to Grant's problem, she could not be sure, but she felt considerably calmer when he left the house half an hour later.

'What do you think?' Grant demanded of her when they faced each other alone in the living-room.

'I think you have a difficult time ahead of you, but you'll make it.'

'Your confidence has always been as unshakeable as a rock.'

Liz suppressed a smile. 'Oh, it shifts and shudders at times, but I'm convinced you're still going to achieve wonderful things as a surgeon.'

'Would it make any difference to you if the operation and the therapy fail to have the desired effect?'

'It will make no difference at all,' she replied at once, a little startled by his question until she recalled how Myra had walked out on him after the accident, and Liz despised her at that precise moment. 'It isn't going to fail, Grant,' she insisted, gripping his arms tightly.

'And even if it does it will make no difference to us—to what we have together.'

She drew his head down to hers and kissed him, but when he did not respond to the touch of her lips she had a peculiar feeling that he had somehow gone beyond her reach, and she turned away from him with a heavy feeling in her breast.

'I think I'll go up to bed,' she said when she reached the door, but Grant seemed not to hear her, and she turned away miserably, crossing the hall, and taking the stairs slowly up to their room.

Liz pretended to be asleep when Grant came to bed an hour later, but her longing for him was too great when his hand touched her shoulder, and she turned into his arms, to the hard warmth of his body, and the magic of his kisses. She hated herself for being so weak, but when his warm, sensual mouth shifted down to the curve of her breast she no longer cared about anything except the fact that he still wanted her and needed her in some strange way.

Grant went into hospital the following afternoon, and Liz spent an awful night alone in that house. After her father's death she had lived alone for six months in Riverside's rambling old house, but it had been her home, and she had been surrounded by familiar objects which had aroused happy memories. Here, in Grant's house, she found nothing to comfort her, and so very much to unnerve her.

She was at the hospital very early in the morning; nothing on earth would have kept her away, and she remained there until Grant was finally wheeled from the theatre back to his ward.

'The operation was a success,' Alan Bishop answered

Liz's query. 'Now it all depends on how well the tendons in his hand respond to therapy.'

'Do you think——'

'I'm not thinking,' Alan interrupted, noticing her troubled expression. 'I'm simply keeping my fingers crossed, and I suggest you do the same.'

Liz nodded, then she quickly followed the direction the orderlies had taken with Grant. He was still under the influence of the anaesthetic when she was finally allowed to see him, and the ward Sister suggested that she go home and return again that afternoon.

She hated having to leave him, but she realised that there was nothing she could do to help him if she remained there at his side, so she drove herself back to the house in Grant's powerful Jaguar. She found the waiting intolerable and, above all, she hated being in that house without Grant. She could never think of it as *her* home. It was Myra's. Myra had chosen the furnishings, Myra had seen to the décor, and . . . oh, God, why was she torturing herself with Myra at that precise moment?

Liz had lunch out on the terrace. She preferred it to eating alone in that large dining-room, and when at last it was time for her to go to the hospital she found herself heavy-footed on the accelerator in her haste. The whining of a traffic policeman's siren finally got through to her, and she reduced speed drastically while she watched him approach on his motorcycle. Her heart was pounding in her mouth, but he sped past without so much as a glance in her direction in his urgency to reach something up ahead in the traffic. Liz laughed at herself, and she felt lightheaded with relief, but she took care not to exceed the speed limit again.

'How do you feel?' she was asking Grant ten minutes later.

'I feel as though someone has used a mallet on my hand,' he said, gritting his teeth against the pain, and she glanced about her searchingly.

'Shouldn't I find the nurse and ask her for something?'

'I was given a painkiller a few minutes before you came,' he grunted, and she took his left hand in both of hers and held it tightly.

'Please come home soon.' She had not meant to say that, but it did not matter to her that he should know she was missing him.

'I didn't think you would miss me so soon,' he mocked her, but she made no attempt to avoid those steel-grey eyes.

'It's lonely there without you, and all those mirrors give me the creeps.'

'You're much more effective than a painkiller,' Grant laughed. 'I think I must arrange for you to stay here.'

Liz did not reply, but in her heart she knew that she would have been quite happy spending the night on the floor beside his bed rather than return to that empty house where Myra's presence lingered so persistently in every room.

The visiting hour was over much too soon, and she got to her feet reluctantly. She leaned over him to kiss him on the cheek, but he turned his head unexpectedly, and their lips met and clung. His hand slid beneath her thick sweater to lie warm against her flesh, and she drew back sharply. A clinical hospital ward was not the place for the emotions that were surging through her at that moment.

'I'll see you this evening,' she said, avoiding his mocking eyes.

'I think not.'

Hurt and bewildered, she asked abruptly, 'Why not?'

'I would prefer it if you didn't travel about after dark.' She started to protest, but Grant silenced her with a terse, 'Don't make me worry about you as well.'

It made sense, of course, but all she could think of were the long hours alone in his house until the following afternoon when she could visit him in hospital. 'Pull yourself together, Liz, you're not a baby,' she admonished herself in silence and, squaring her shoulders, she said with forced brightness, 'See you tomorrow, then.'

She walked out of the private ward with her head held high, and almost collided with a tall, lean man in the passage. She was aware of sparkling green eyes looking her up and down, but his glance was appreciative without being insolent.

'This is Dr Grant Battersby's ward, isn't it?' he enquired a little hesitantly.

'That's right.'

'I'm Joe Townsend,' he introduced himself.

'Liz Battersby,' she responded, and he studied her a little more closely.

'Are you a relative . . . or something?'

'I'm his wife.'

'His *wife*?' The man's jaw dropped before he collected himself. 'Forgive me if I seem a little surprised, but I had no idea Grant had married while he was up in Pietersburg.'

'You're forgiven,' Liz smiled, deciding that she liked him.

'Look, I must see Grant about something, but will

you wait for me in the foyer?' He noticed her hesitant manner, and explained hastily, 'I'm an old friend of Grant's, since our varsity days.'

Liz relaxed and nodded. 'I'll wait.'

She seated herself gingerly on the hard, wooden bench in the foyer, and waited. What could Joe Townsend want with her? she wondered curiously, and she was still waiting patiently for an explanation fifteen minutes later. She glanced at the clock against the wall and frowned, but a few minutes later the sound of approaching footsteps made her look up to see Joe Townsend coming towards her.

'I'm sorry I kept you waiting, but my business with Grant took a little longer than I'd expected,' he explained with a rueful grin as she rose to her feet and, taking her arm, he accompanied her out to where she had parked the Jaguar. 'Will you have dinner with me this evening?'

Startled by his unexpected invitation, she said mockingly, 'I thought you said you were Grant's friend?'

Joe's smile widened. 'I have permission to take you to dinner.'

'Really?' Her back went rigid. 'Did he suggest it?'

'I asked him.'

'I see.'

She relaxed and felt a little less like a parcel being palmed off on to someone for safe keeping.

'Having dinner with me would be preferable to sitting alone at home, wouldn't it?'

Those green, sparkling eyes surveyed her intently. He had knowingly or unknowingly struck the right chord, and the corners of her mouth lifted in a smile. 'You've persuaded me.'

'Good,' he said abruptly, holding the car door open

for her so that she could slide into the driver's seat. 'Shall I call for you at seven?'

'That would be fine,' she agreed, turning the key in the ignition as he closed the door and stepped back.

'Till this evening, then.'

When she passed through the gates of the hospital grounds Joe Townsend was still standing where she had left him. He waved and she waved back, and she decided yet again that she liked him. He seemed harmless enough, she told herself, and if Grant had agreed that she could have dinner with Joe this evening, then she obviously had nothing to worry about.

Liz took her time preparing herself for her appointment with Joe Townsend that evening, but somehow she was ready long before seven o'clock. The silence in the house was oppressive, she wanted to get away from it, and most of all she was missing Grant. The mirrors against the living-room walls reflected her edginess, and no matter how much she tried she could not avoid seeing herself. She felt like throwing something at her mirror image, but that would not solve anything, and she found herself laughing softly to herself when the words of an old fairy tale came to mind.

Mirror, mirror on the wall
Who is the fairest of us all?

The answer would undoubtedly be *Myra Cavendish*, and Liz groaned inwardly at the thought of what would happen if Myra should return.

Joe Townsend arrived promptly at seven, and when he was shown into the living-room he found Liz waiting almost anxiously for him.

'Am I late?' he asked, his friendly, interested glance travelling over her.

'I'm early,' she confessed without hesitation.

His glance sharpened. 'Something tells me you dislike this place as much as I do.'

So he felt that way about it too, she thought, and the discovery seemed to forge a bond between them.

'Shall we go?' she asked, and a sparkle of mischief leapt into his eyes.

'My carriage is waiting, madam,' he informed her with a sweeping gesture of his hand.

It was going to be a pleasant evening, she knew it, she told herself, but some sixth sense warned her not to be too sure of that.

It was a fifteen-minute drive into the city, but the conversation flowed between them with an ease which surprised Liz. Nothing personal was discussed, and they kept it strictly lighthearted. They seemed to laugh a lot about silly little things, and she found herself relaxing so completely in his company that she eventually found it difficult to believe that she had not known this man longer than a few hours.

The restaurant was crowded, but Joe had fortunately reserved a table and, as the evening progressed, Liz began to study him more closely. She guessed his age to be the same as Grant's, but he looked considerably younger. There was no sign of grey in the crisp, reddish-brown hair, and he laughed a great deal more than Grant did these days.

Grant ... it was difficult to drag her thoughts away from him. Was he still suffering the painful after-effects of the operation that morning? Was he thinking of her? Would they allow him to come home soon?

'How long have you known Grant?' Joe asked, almost as if he had guessed the direction her thoughts had taken, and she looked up from her dessert to smile at him.

'I've known Grant practically all my life. Our farm is . . . *was* next door to his in the Pietersburg district.'

Joe studied her intently for a moment, then he shook his head as if something puzzled him. 'You're not the type of woman I thought he would marry.'

'You mean I'm not like Myra?' she voiced what she guessed was in his mind, and his discomfort told her that she had guessed correctly.

'You know about her?'

'Myra was in the same grade at school as my sister Stacy who's six years older than I am.'

'You've known about her all along, then?'

'It was on our farm, more than six years ago, that she met him,' she replied distastefully.

Joe had something on his mind, and Liz sensed it when he spoke. 'Grant's a brilliant surgeon, and in every other way a shrewd, clever man,' he said thoughtfully, 'but where Myra was concerned he was as blind as a bat. He became totally obsessed with her, and she could do almost as she pleased with him. He wanted to marry her, but Myra was not the type to settle for one man. She wanted to be free; for Grant, and for any other man who might be foolish enough to fall for her particular brand of beauty and charm.'

'So they lived together,' Liz drove the sword into her own heart.

'Not exactly,' Joe contradicted her. 'Grant bought that house a year ago and gave Myra a free hand with the décor. I can't say for sure whether that helped to change her mind, but she finally agreed to marry him—only to drop him like a hot potato when it was thought that his career as a noted surgeon was at an end and, as far as I know, Grant only moved into that house after she'd left him.'

Liz felt her insides jerk. Was it shock . . . or relief? She could not be sure. 'Are you telling me that they never actually lived there together?'

'Myra lived there for some months, but Grant continued to occupy his flat in Hillbrow.' Joe smiled wryly. 'If they were having an affair, then they were very discreet about it.'

A load had suddenly been lifted off her mind. She had imagined them living together in that house all these years, but now the picture looked considerably brighter.

'Tell me about yourself, Joe,' she changed the subject. 'Are you a doctor as well?'

'Nothing quite so glamorous, I'm afraid,' he laughed. 'My speciality is law.'

'That's interesting,' she said, leaning her elbow on the table and cupping her chin in her palm so that the candlelight danced in her eyes. 'Apart from being a friend of Grant's, do you also handle his legal affairs?'

'That's right,' he smiled, then he gestured towards her empty glass. 'More wine?'

'No, thank you,' she shook her head. 'I think I've had enough for one night.'

'Do you love Grant?'

His question was as unexpected as a jab in the midriff, and she was temporarily winded, but the moment she got her breath back she said coolly, 'I wouldn't have married him for any other reason.'

'How does he feel about Myra these days?'

'It's not a subject we discuss,' she said abruptly, removing her elbow off the table, and fiddling unnecessarily with her table napkin.

'He's made it taboo, has he?' Joe persisted shrewdly.

'Yes,' she shifted uncomfortably. 'He said she belonged in the past.'

'Liz, there's something I think you ought to know.' She looked up then, and his grave expression chilled her. 'Myra's back in Johannesburg. She arrived yesterday.'

The coldness spread, clutching at her heart like an icy, clammy hand. 'Does Grant know?' she croaked.

'If he does, then I certainly haven't been the one to tell him,' Joe set her mind at rest on that score.

'Do you think she'll make an effort to contact him?'

'What do you think?'

She could see the pity in his eyes, and it made her flinch inwardly. 'But if she finds out that he's married——'

'My dear, a marriage licence has never stopped Myra in the past from getting what she wants,' Joe interrupted her, his hand finding hers across the table. 'How sure are you of Grant's feelings for you?'

Liz wished with all her heart that she could have said 'He loves me', but that was something she would never have the privilege of saying. Perhaps he had learned to care for her a little, but then he never gave any sign that he felt anything more for her than desire and, lowering her eyes, she said miserably, 'I'm not very sure at all how he—he feels about me.'

'Will you promise me one thing?' Joe's fingers tightened about hers. 'Will you come to me if you ever find yourself in need of assistance?'

'You're very kind.'

He released her hand and took something out of his wallet. 'Here's my card if you ever have to contact me in a hurry.'

He took her home some minutes later, and although he declined her offer to make him something to drink, he accompanied her into the hall. Liz thanked him very nicely, but she had a feeling that he was not listening as he took her chin between his fingers and tipped her face up to his.

'You have lovely eyes, Liz,' he said softly. 'They're the kind a man could drown himself in, and if Grant can't see in them what I see, then he's a bigger fool than I would have thought and deserves no better than the Myras of this world.'

'You've succeeded in boosting my morale,' she laughed off his remark.

'I'm serious,' he insisted, dropping his hand to his side.

'Goodnight, Joe, and thank you once again for taking me out to dinner,' she changed the subject.

'What about tomorrow evening?' he persisted with an eagerness that disturbed her.

'I think not,' she shook her head. 'But thanks for asking.'

His disappointment was evident, but he accepted her decision, and moments later she was alone with fear and uncertainty as her only companions for the night.

Grant was released from hospital on the Saturday, but the therapy did not start until almost two weeks later, and Liz accompanied him whenever he went for these therapeutic sessions. She was afraid to let him out of her sight; afraid that Myra might hatch out somewhere unexpectedly, and afraid of how Grant would react to her. Did he know? Had he heard? She wished that she could ask him, but she did not have the nerve somehow.

The weeks passed, taking them into one of those cold winters on the reef, and in time Liz gradually began to shake off her fears. If Myra was in Johannesburg, then she was staying out of their way, and Liz prayed desperately that she would continue to do so.

It was mid-July before Grant could return to his consulting-rooms in the city. The operation and the therapy had been a tremendous success, and to celebrate this fact he took Liz out to dinner one evening. His spirits were high, and so were hers. She was happy, so terribly happy for his sake, and she made no secret of it.

'It was your rock-like confidence that kept me going,' he told her quite bluntly.

'Nonsense,' she laughed it off. 'I knew you had enough self-determination to see you through all the difficult moments.'

'Liz . . .' his hand found hers across the table, 'I haven't exactly been the best husband a girl could wish for.'

'I won't deny there's room for improvement,' she teased, her eyes dancing with mirth.

'I wish I could give you more.'

The laughter died slowly in her eyes. 'Is it so very difficult to care for me a little?'

'I do care for you, Liz.' His smile was mocking and intensely sensual. 'Haven't I shown you lately how much I care?'

She looked away from him, her colour deepening. 'Must you always reduce everything to a physical level?'

'The physical side of our marriage is what interests me most,' he mocked her mercilessly. 'Who would believe me if I told them that behind that cool, down-to-earth, country-faced exterior there lurked an intelligent and passionate woman?'

'Stop it, Grant!' she begged, her face burning.

'Can I help it if it's the truth?' he persisted, raising her hand to his lips regardless of whether people were watching them in the crowded restaurant, and she felt embarrassingly certain that they were.

Some *had* been watching, but Liz only discovered this when they had had their dinner and were lingering over their coffee.

In the far corner of the restaurant a tall, slender woman detached herself from a group of diners, and she moved with a practised grace. She was elegantly dressed in the latest fashion, and her tawny-coloured hair had been cut and styled into a sleek cap to accentuate the flawless complexion of her classic features. Her beauty was attracting attention, and she revelled in it, but Liz felt as if the air was slowly being squeezed from her lungs as she watched Myra Cavendish approach their table. Soon, *very* soon, Grant would see her, and then . . .!

'Oh, God . . . help me!' Liz prayed silently, but nothing happened, Myra kept coming like an avalanche; inevitable, unavoidable, and totally destructive.

Liz wished she could reach out to throw a protective shield around Grant, but it was too late. He turned for some reason, saw Myra, and went as white as the pillar behind him.

'Darling!' Myra breathed seductively, subsiding very elegantly on to the curved bench beside Grant, and placing a slender, possessive hand on his arm. 'I've been watching you for the past hour, but I couldn't get away until now. You're looking simply marvellous,

Grant, and I believe you're quite well again.'

'Liz can vouch for that,' said Grant, staccato-voiced.

'Liz?' Recognition dawned in those slanted green eyes as Myra acknowledged Liz's presence at last. 'I've been trying to place you, but now, of course, I realise who you are. You're Liz Holden—Stacy's little sister. Are you visiting here in Johannesburg?'

'Liz is my wife,' Grant cut in abruptly before Liz could reply.

'Your wife?' Myra laughed with an incredulity that rankled. 'Darling, you must be joking. You couldn't possibly have married anyone so—so young. Why, it's almost indecent!'

Liz opened her mouth, but Grant, beat her to it again with a terse, 'Whichever way you would like to look at it, Myra, we've been married for more than three months.'

'Well, congratulations,' Myra smiled derisively, her eyes spitting pure venom at Liz before she turned to Grant with a note of intimacy in her voice. 'I shall keep in touch. We have so much to catch up on, don't we, darling?'

Myra left their table to return to her friends, and Liz could not help recalling Joe Townsend's remark. 'A marriage licence has never stopped Myra in the past from getting what she wants.' And Myra wanted Grant. It made no difference to her that she had left him in the lurch when he had needed her most. She had had him once, and she was confident that she could have him again.

A thin film of perspiration stood out on Grant's forehead, and the hand that held the glass was shaking. He looked like an addict in need of a vital shot in the arm, and Myra was the one who could give it to him. Liz watched him in silence while he made an obvious effort to control himself, and never before had she felt so utterly helpless, and so sick inside with fear. The wine had gone sour, and the celebration had become a farce.

'Let's go,' she said stiffly, and Grant nodded in agreement.

They tried to make conversation on the way home, but they both failed. To Liz it felt as if she was with a stranger who had erected a barrier between them which was impenetrable, and that barrier was *Myra*.

Grant poured himself a stiff whisky when they arrived at the house, and he was pouring the second when Liz finally said goodnight and went up to bed. She could not sleep, not with Grant downstairs in the living-room, drinking, or whatever it was he was doing.

It was long after midnight when at last he entered their bedroom. He undressed himself in the dark, muttering a few curses when he bumped into something, but Liz pretended to be asleep even though she was painfully aware of every movement he made.

When she could no longer hear him moving about she waited for the familiar weight of his body beside her on the bed, but nothing happened. She turned over on to her back, her eyes searching the moonlit darkness, and she saw him standing silhouetted against the window as if he were staring out into the blackness beyond. What was he thinking? Oh, God, he couldn't still want her after everything they had been to each other these past months! Could he? she asked herself the agonising question.

She passed a shaking hand over her cold face and

slipped quietly out of bed. 'Grant?' She touched his arm lightly and felt the muscles tense beneath her fingers. 'It's so late. Won't you come to bed?'

For a moment he seemed not to hear her, then he stirred and turned towards her, his eyes on her pale face in the filtered moonlight coming in through the window. Her hair was dishevelled, and she was unaware of how young and vulnerable she looked standing there before him in her lacy nightdress with her heart throbbing so painfully in her breast. *Love you, love you!* The words cried out from the depths of her soul, keeping time with the rhythmic beat of her heart, and Grant seemed to come alive to the silent appeal in the hands she held out to him.

They went to bed without speaking, but when their bodies touched Liz felt him shudder, and he made love to her that night with a strange desperation that kept her awake until dawn with desolation and despair tearing away at her insides.

CHAPTER EIGHT

THAT meeting in the restaurant with Myra Cavendish changed the course of their lives drastically. Grant became withdrawn, and flung himself back into his work as if his life depended on it. He came home late in the evenings, and often stayed out until the early hours of the morning, but what hurt Liz most was when he moved into the room adjoining theirs. He used pressure of work as an excuse for his late hours, and insisted that he did not want to disturb her at night, but Liz knew she would be a fool to believe that. She tried once to discuss the situation with him, but he became so infuriated with her that she was too afraid to mention the subject again. She could not prove that he was seeing Myra, but she imagined he was, and it kept her awake most nights until deep shadows appeared beneath her eyes.

Grant's behaviour was not the only thing that troubled Liz at that time. She was beginning to suspect that she was pregnant. It was something neither of them had taken into consideration, and although they had taken a few precautionary measures, there had been times when precaution had been the last thing on their minds. She had no idea how Grant felt about having children, but she hoped that, if her suspicions were confirmed, it would help considerably towards stabilising their marriage. Perhaps a child was what they needed to help him shake free of this dreadful hold Myra had on him again.

Another long week passed; a week of wondering, hoping, and praying, but the true gravity of the situation was made clear to her when she looked up from her sewing one afternoon to find that she was no longer alone in the living-room.

'Myra!' Liz gasped the woman's name in astonishment.

'You don't mind my coming in unannounced, do you?' Green eyes darted about the room and, not giving Liz an opportunity to speak, she added: 'I still think of this place as my own.'

'I'm sure you do,' Liz said coldly, regaining her composure as she watched Myra sit down and fold her legs elegantly.

'I'm glad to see that everything is still as I left it,' Myra smiled that cold, humourless smile while she glanced about her once more.

'Everything is still the same except for the small lounge across the hall which I use as a study.' Their glances clashed in battle. 'Why are you here, Myra?'

'I should have remembered you're not the type to beat about the bush,' Myra smiled sweetly, but the sweetness was mixed with venom. 'Stacy always said you would risk the fires of hell rather than walk around them.'

'Get to the point.'

'I want Grant.'

Liz felt the shock of her words right down into her toes. The sparring was over, and their daggers were drawn. 'What makes you think that I'm going to let you have him?'

'You'll have no choice.'

'You're very sure of yourself?'

'I'm sure of Grant.' Myra drew blood.

'You had him once, but when he needed you most you left him in the lurch,' Liz parried.

'I was in a state of shock after his accident, and I admit quite freely that I behaved like a fool.' Myra raised her beautifully arched eyebrows at Liz's sceptical expression. 'We all make mistakes, darling. I've admitted mine, so why don't you admit that you made a grave mistake when you decided to marry Grant?'

'As far as I'm concerned, Myra, our marriage was not a mistake.'

'He doesn't love you.'

Liz winced inwardly as Myra drew blood a second time. 'I know he doesn't love me.'

'Why hold on to him, then?'

'Grant asked me to marry him,' Liz replied evenly. 'If he wants his freedom, then he has only to ask for it.'

'Why make it difficult and awkward for him, *and* for yourself?' Myra sighed. 'Why not simply admit defeat and quietly disappear out of his life?'

'That may be your solution, but it's not mine. I don't walk out, or turn my back on my commitments.'

Liz scored a hit. It was two to one, and that flash of anger in Myra's heavily lashed eyes told her so.

'Suit yourself,' Myra shrugged lightly, 'but don't say you haven't been warned.'

They sat there, mentally circling each other, but both equally determined not to give the other an opening.

'Was there anything else?' Liz asked coolly.

'No,' Myra smiled, admiring herself unashamedly in the mirrors. 'I'm looking forward, though, to moving in here with Grant.'

That was a hit below the belt. Myra was fighting

dirty as Pamela had warned in her letter, but she was scoring points nevertheless.

Liz put her sewing aside, and rose to her feet with an unconscious grace and dignity which came to her as naturally as breathing. 'You know your way out.'

'Don't be nasty, darling,' Myra sneered, uncurling herself from the chair, and overpowering Liz with her exotic perfume. 'You surely didn't think yourself capable of holding him, did you?'

Her disparaging glance swept Liz up and down, but instead of anger Liz felt a strange calmness rising within her. 'You're beautiful, Myra, no one can dispute that fact, but your beauty is limited only to the outside, and some day soon Grant is going to see you as you really are—a selfish, heartless shell with nothing to commend you except a body that pleases, and in time you'll lose that as well.'

Liz scored a triple, and now they were even. Most people possessed an Achilles' heel, that tender spot where they were most vulnerable, and Myra's was her beauty. She was obsessed with it, and Liz had always known that she was intensely afraid of losing it. Liz despised herself for striking out in such a despicable way, but Myra had laid down the rules, and Liz had followed.

'Grant will never escape me, my dear. I have only to snap my fingers and he'll come running,' Myra hissed, and her face was distorted with fury. 'Just wait, and you'll see!'

It was only when the outer door slammed behind Myra's departing figure that Liz felt her calmness desert her. Her legs started to shake, then her entire body, and she sat down heavily in her chair to stare with sightless eyes at the shaggy carpet beneath her feet.

Grant would never leave her for someone like Myra. Could he possibly be that much of a fool? Surely their marriage meant *something* to him? Liz tried to convince herself that, whatever the cause of the problem between Grant and herself, it could be ironed out in time, but that did not diminish the fact that Myra was so frighteningly sure of herself. 'I have only to snap my fingers and he'll come running.' That was precisely how sure Myra was of herself.

Liz snapped her fingers, absently imitating Myra's furious actions, and quite suddenly she was laughing a little hysterically, but she clamped down on it swiftly. She tried to convince herself that she had nothing to fear, that Myra was merely desperate in her attempts to win Grant back, and she succeeded partially. There was, after all, something else which needed her immediate attention.

Two days later Liz drove herself into the city to keep her appointment that afternoon with the doctor. The little green Mini which Grant had bought her shortly after his release from the hospital manoeuvred easily in the busy Johannesburg streets, and parking was no problem when she arrived at the medical centre.

Liz felt nervous when she found herself ushered into the doctor's rooms half an hour later, but he was a kindly gentleman in his late fifties, and he fortunately did not associate her with Grant when she gave him her name. The examination lasted only a few minutes and, when she faced the doctor once again across the wide expanse of his desk, he smiled at her.

'Your suspicions were correct,' he said. 'I would say you're at least eight weeks pregnant.'

'Are you sure?' she asked with growing excitement.

'I'm positive.' His smile broadened. 'You may go home, Mrs Battersby, and tell your husband that he's going to become a father in the not too distant future.'

Liz tightened her fingers on the strap of her handbag to steady the trembling of her hands. 'Thank you, I'll do that.'

'Come and see me again in a month's time,' he said, accompanying her to the door, and Liz nodded without speaking.

She felt too shaky to venture into the traffic immediately. There was a tea-room across the street, and she fastened her coat buttons to keep out the cold while she waited for the traffic lights to change. A few minutes later she was sitting at a table with a hot cup of tea in front of her while she tried to analyse her feelings. She felt excited and afraid simultaneously, but the knowledge that she was pregnant filled her mostly with awe. There was a new life growing inside her; a life which Grant had as much a share in as she, and suddenly she could not wait to tell him. She drank her tea quickly, almost scalding her mouth in the process, and then she was hurrying out of the tea-room and across the street to where her Mini was parked. Everything else was temporarily forgotten, shifted to the recesses of her mind to make way for this new and exciting development, and Liz made up her mind that, when she arrived at the house, she would contact Grant somehow and beg him, if necessary, to be home in time for dinner that evening. She wanted to tell him, she wanted to share her secret with him before . . .! No, she would not think of it now. Later perhaps, but not now.

Grant's sleek white Jaguar was parked in the sweeping, circular driveway when Liz arrived at the house, and she stared at it in surprise. Was it a good or a bad omen? She did not stop to decide, and hurried into the house as quickly as she could. She found him in the living-room, slumped uncharacteristically in a chair with a cigarette dangling between his lips.

'Grant, I'm so glad you're home early. I have——' She stopped abruptly, pausing also in her happy flight across the room when he rose from his chair and turned to face her. Their eyes met, and the atmosphere was suddenly crackling with an awful tension. 'What is it? What's wrong?' she heard herself asking without actually being conscious that she had spoken.

He gestured towards the cabinet against the wall. 'Would you like a drink?'

Her eyes shifted to the clock on the mantelshelf. 'Four o'clock in the afternoon is a bit early for me.'

'You won't mind if I have one?'

She shook her head slowly and watched him pour himself a whisky. 'What's on your mind?'

He did not answer her at once and simply stood staring at the glass in his hand, then he swallowed down its contents in one gulp, and turned to her. 'It was never my intention to hurt you, Liz, and you must believe that, but there's no nice way of saying what I have to.'

'It's Myra Cavendish, isn't it?' she was saying in a voice that was surprisingly calm considering that her insides were shaking so uncontrollably.

'Yes, it is.'

Shock swept through her like an icy blast of wind across the highveld. She had been warned, but the reality was still a tremendous blow.

'I should have seen it coming since that night we met her in the restaurant,' she whispered, her eyes searching his face, then she controlled herself and asked bluntly, 'Are you having an affair?'

'Credit me with a sense of decency, Liz,' he replied angrily. 'We've met, and we've talked, that's all.'

'Did she tell you that she wanted me to simply fade out of your life to make it easier for both of you?'

His glance sharpened. 'She came to see you?'

'A few days ago.' Liz drew a careful, steadying breath and explained. 'At the time I thought she was merely trying to frighten me, but I should have known she was serious.'

'I'm sorry about that,' he said, and he looked it too, she thought charitably, but the room was beginning to sway about her. 'Are you all right?' he asked quickly, stretching out a hand to steady her and lower her into a chair.

'Yes ... yes, I'm ... fine ... I think.' *I must not faint. Oh, God, I must not faint*, she thought anxiously, and fortunately the room righted itself again within a few seconds. 'Did she explain her reasons for walking out on you after the accident?'

'She did.'

'And you believed her?' she demanded cynically, and Grant's brow darkened with anger.

'I had no reason not to believe her.'

'And how did you explain the reason for our marriage?' she asked, unable to hide the bitterness welling up inside her. 'Did you tell her that I was only too eager to help you pass the time until she decided to come back to you?'

'For God's sake, Liz, I——'

'That's what our marriage has amounted to, hasn't it?' she interrupted bitingly.

'You must remember that I asked you to marry me

at a time when I was at my lowest ebb, mentally and physically,' said Grant, and Liz wondered curiously why she felt no pain, only an icy numbness where her heart ought to be.

'What you're trying to say is that you knew Myra wouldn't have you under those circumstances and I was better than nothing at all.'

'Dammit, Liz, it wasn't like that at all!' he growled, going faintly white about the mouth.

'Do you want a divorce?'

His mouth tightened, but his eyes had a glazed look that troubled her. 'I don't know yet what I want. All I know at the moment is that I need to be free to sort myself out.'

'Then that settles it, doesn't it?' Liz said bitterly, getting to her feet and surprised that her legs continued to hold her in an upright position.

'Please try to understand, Liz,' he muttered, crushing his cigarette into the ashtray and shaking his head.

'I'll pack and leave at once,' she said, turning towards the door, but Grant's hand on her arm checked her.

'You don't have to leave—not yet, anyway.'

'*Don't touch me!*' she wanted to shout, but instead she stared down at his bronzed hand with the fine scars on the back and said calmly, 'I would prefer it this way, and you'll be absolutely free to decide whether you want a divorce or not.'

'Where will you go?'

'Does it matter?' she shrugged, disengaging her arm from his clasp.

'Of course it matters!' his harsh voice scraped along her raw nerves. 'I can't simply let you go off without knowing that you'll be safe.'

Her chin rose defiantly. 'I can look after myself.'

'Liz!' he groaned, pushing agitated fingers through his hair and making it stand on end in an endearing manner. 'Where will you spend the night?'

'I'll move into a hotel, and in the morning I shall have decided where to go,' she relented, walking stiffly away from him, but at the door she paused and turned. 'She doesn't love you, you know. She never has, and she never will.'

He looked away, the muscles jutting out savagely along the side of his jaw. 'That's none of your business!'

Shut out, with the door slammed securely in her face, she felt herself dying inside as she reeled mentally beneath that searing stab of pain. She had asked for it, and she had got it exactly where it had hurt most.

'I'd appreciate it if you would arrange for a taxi to call for me in an hour's time.'

Grant glanced at her sharply. 'You have the Mini.'

'*No!*' she snapped, recoiling from the idea of taking something from this man who no longer wanted her.

'It was a gift.' His hands bit into her shoulders, giving pain and pleasure, and filling her with a longing so intense that she very nearly gave way to it, but she was prevented from flinging herself into his arms when he released her and said abruptly, 'It would please me very much if you would keep it.'

His words triggered off a thought. She had tried so very hard to please him, but perhaps she had tried too hard, and should have demanded more. She had given of herself unstintingly, and he had taken. The things he had given her were of material value, such as the Mini, and it was with a surge of bitterness that she decided to keep it.

'Thank you,' she murmured her acceptance, then she left him there in the living-room, and went upstairs.

Liz packed automatically, not caring very much how she bundled her things into the suitcase. Grant had shied away from the suggestion of a divorce, but there was no doubt in her mind that he would eventually get around to it. She wished she could cry, but there were no tears, only this deadly cold feeling inside that filled her with an aching numbness. The tears would come later, she told herself. When there was no possibility of Grant walking in on her she would cry her heart out, but not yet . . . *not yet*!

An hour later she summoned one of the servants to carry her suitcases down to the car, but her typewriter and the manuscript she had been working on she took herself. She was ready to leave, and all that remained was to say goodbye to Grant.

She found him in the living-room where she had left him, and he was standing in front of the fireplace with a drink in his hand, staring broodingly down into the empty grate. 'I can't take everything with me now, but I'll let you have my address as soon as I'm settled, then the rest of my things can be railed on to me.' Was that calm, clear voice actually hers? she wondered in a detached sort of way. 'Goodbye, Grant.'

His hand clasped hers, its warmth dispersing some of the iciness in her veins, and she glimpsed again that peculiar glazed look in his grey eyes. 'Liz, I'm sorry.'

'So am I.' She tried to smile, but her face remained rigid. She wanted to add something terribly clever, perhaps even spiteful, but all she could do was stare at him dumbly.

She drew her hand from his, and walked away from him without a backward glance; she dared not look back if she did not want him to see the pain and despair in her eyes, and a few minutes later she was driving away from the house of mirrors which would soon be reflecting the image Grant longed to see.

Liz spent the night in a hotel, but she spent most of those long hours on a chair beside the window, staring blankly at the building across the street with its flashing coloured lights. She thought of calling Joe Townsend, but decided against it. He would hear from Grant soon enough, and she could not really bear to see anyone just yet.

She shivered in the air-conditioned warmth of the room, and drew her robe more firmly about her. Her hand brushed across her flat stomach, and then she remembered. She was going to have a baby! She was taking something with her which Grant knew nothing about; something which would fill the loneliness and emptiness of the future. Grant had, after all, given her something which would make living worthwhile. A lump rose into her throat, but it subsided again almost at once. She felt so calm; so terribly calm that it was almost frightening, but sleep continued to evade her, and she eventually watched the wintry sun rise over the rooftops of the buildings.

Liz took the journey to Pietersburg in easy stages. She stopped for tea, and stopped for lunch even though she hardly touched her food, and it was almost three o'clock that afternoon before she pulled into Stacy's driveway.

'Liz!' Stacy exclaimed when she opened the door and found Liz standing there. 'Good heavens, we thought we were never going to hear from you, let alone see you.'

'Do you think you could put me up for a week or so?' Liz asked, allowing Stacy to draw her into the house.

'Darling, we'd love to have you.' Stacy called one of the servants and instructed them to collect the suitcases from the Mini, then she turned back to Liz. 'I'll have your things taken up to the spare room.'

'Thanks, Stacy.'

'You look all in,' Stacy observed, staring hard at Liz as they crossed the hall and walked down the short passage into the kitchen.

'I am rather tired,' Liz admitted, but it was much more than that. She was beginning to feel as if a bus had gone over her.

'A cup of strong tea, that's what you need,' Stacy announced brightly, but the frown did not leave her brow as she studied Liz's white, drawn face with the dark smudges beneath lacklustre eyes.

'How's Rosalie?' Liz asked tiredly, seating herself at the table while Stacy made the tea.

'You won't know her, she's grown so much.'

'I suppose she's asleep?'

'Yes,' Stacy smiled, 'but when you've had your tea you may go up and take a peep at her.'

Liz did not argue, she was too tired at that moment to do much more than sit there and drink the tea Stacy placed before her. Later, when she went upstairs, she did not linger too long beside the cradle where the chubby little girl lay sleeping with her rosy lips pouting almost as if she were inviting a kiss.

'Lie down and rest for a while,' Stacy insisted, but, when they stood facing each other in the room Liz had occupied before her marriage to Grant, Stacy stared at her sister intently and asked: 'What's wrong, my dear?'

Liz sat down heavily on the bed, her hands moving restlessly in her lap. 'It's over.'

'You mean your marriage?' Stacy queried, paling slightly when she sat down beside Liz.

'Myra came back, and Grant . . .' Liz drew a deep, tired breath. 'I think he's seriously considering a divorce.'

'He wants to marry Myra, after the way she treated him?' Stacy demanded in a shocked, incredulous voice.

'I—I think he loves her.'

Her words echoed hollowly in the silent room, and it was as if she had become detached from herself. She was listening to someone else speak, and she was feeling none of that person's pain.

Stacy would have had every right to say 'I told you so', but it would have been totally against her nature, Liz realised when her sister simply asked quietly, 'What are you going to do?'

'I'll find myself a flat somewhere, and write, and . . .' A flicker of emotion darted across her face for the first time, and she raised cold hands to her equally cold cheeks. 'Oh, God, Stacy! I'm going to have his child!' she whispered hoarsely.

'Does he know that?'

'I only saw the doctor yesterday, and——'

'You were going to tell him last night, but he beat you to it by asking for his freedom,' Stacy filled in for her shrewdly when she paused abruptly, and when Liz nodded, she said: 'You should have told him.'

'And what kind of marriage would I have had then, with a husband who'd decided to stay with me simply because I was going to have his child?' Liz demanded distastefully, letting her hands fall listlessly back into her lap. 'No, oh, *no*! I couldn't have tolerated that!'

Stacy's brown eyes mirrored deep concern. 'You seem to be taking it all so calmly.'

'I'll have his child, and no one can take that away from me.'

They stared at each other for a moment without speaking, then Stacy urged Liz to lie down and rest before dinner that evening.

'We'll talk again later,' she said, then she went out of the room, closing the door softly behind her.

Liz felt tired; so terribly, terribly tired, but she could not sleep. She unpacked her suitcases, taking her time, keeping herself occupied, and above all trying not to think. It was over, and that was that. No tears, no sighs, no regrets, and . . . oh, God, why did she feel so dead inside?

She heard Angus arrive home that evening, and when she went downstairs a few minutes later it was obvious that Stacy had told him what had happened. He simply put his arms around Liz, gave her a brotherly kiss on the cheek, and muttered in his gruff voice, 'We'll take care of you, lass.'

Liz found that her facial muscles were beginning to work again, and she smiled up at him briefly, accepting the glass of sherry he handed to her. She sipped at it, and it warmed her insides. The blood flowed a little more strongly through her veins, and her cheeks regained a little colour.

Angus and Stacy kept the conversation going all evening, but Liz contributed very little to it, and at the dinner table she did no more than rearrange her food on her plate. When she tried to eat the food lodged uncomfortably in her throat, so she finally gave up the effort, and settled for a cup of coffee instead.

'Shall I give you something to help you sleep?' Stacy offered when Liz eventually said goodnight, but Liz shook her head.

'I'll be all right, thank you.'

Strangely enough Liz did sleep. She went into a deep, dreamless sleep from which she awoke around midnight with severe pains in the lower half of her body. She tried to get up to take a few aspirins, but the stab of pain that shot through her was so intense that she gasped and fell back on to the bed, clutching one of the pillows against her and curling herself up into a tight ball as the waves of pain washed over her. She might have cried out, she could not remember, the next moment Stacy was standing beside the bed.

'Liz, what is it?'

'The pain!' she groaned through clenched teeth. 'Oh, Stacy, the *pain!*'

'Lie still!' Stacy ordered sharply. 'I'm going to call Angus, and we're taking you straight to the hospital.'

It could only have been a matter of minutes, but it felt more like hours before Stacy returned with Angus. They wrapped Liz in a blanket, and Angus carried her out of the house to the car with Stacy almost running to keep up with him.

'Stacy?' Liz gasped when the waves of pain became more acute soon after Angus had set the car in motion.

'Try to relax, darling,' Stacy whispered urgently, wiping away the perspiration on Liz's forehead. 'Everything's going to be all right.'

It was all very well to be told to relax, and that everything would be all right, but how did one cope with an agonising pain which seemed to be tearing her insides apart? Liz was beginning to suspect what was happening to her, and she clenched her teeth, praying harder than she had ever prayed before. 'Please, God! Please don't take my baby away from me! It's all I'll have; the only tangible thing left of what was once a lovely dream. *Please, God!*'

Angus must have broken all the speed limits getting Liz to the hospital, and after that everything was a fast-moving blur which Liz observed through a red mist of pain. She was aware of voices, motion, lights, a pin-prick in her arm, and then mercifully nothing more except that feeling that she was drifting beyond herself, and beyond her pain on to a realm where nothing could touch her.

When Liz came to her senses much later she was lying in a hospital bed with the night light switched on above her head. She felt battered and bruised, and reluctant to surface from that peaceful plain, but someone was holding on to her hand and calling her name softly. She turned her head, and found herself looking up into eyes filled with compassion, and traces of recent tears.

'Stacy?' Liz whispered anxiously, and then there was a sinking feeling in her breast when she realised what she was doing there.

'Liz, I'm sorry,' Stacy said softly.

'I've lost the baby, haven't I?'

It was a senseless question. Why else would she feel so bruised inside, and for what other reason would Stacy sit there looking at her with so much sympathy and compassion in her tearful eyes?

'They did everything they possibly could,' Stacy told her.

'*Oh, God, why?*' Liz groaned, fighting against an

agonising pain of a different nature. '*Why* did I have to lose it?'

'It was shock, Liz. The doctor explained that it happens sometimes when one has received a severe shock, and your body simply rejected the baby.'

How simple it sounded ... how clinical! Shock! Rejection! Words in a dictionary which meant nothing at all until they touched you personally. Grant had practically asked her for a divorce, he no longer wanted her ... shock! And the ultimate conclusion was ... rejection! But why did it have to be that way? She had wanted this baby so much. *So very much!*

'There's nothing left now, is there?'

Stacy's fingers tightened about hers. 'I think I should telephone Grant, and——'

'No!' Liz reacted violently to the suggestion, her eyes dark pools of anguish in her pale face. 'It's over—it's finished! I never want to hear his name mentioned again, and I never want to see him again for as long as I live!'

'Liz ...'

'*I mean it, Stacy!*'

'If that's what you want, darling, then that's how it shall be,' Stacy replied soothingly. 'What you need now is rest, and plenty of it, so close your eyes and try to sleep.'

'I am rather tired,' Liz confessed, but she knew she would not sleep. 'Is Angus still here?'

'He went home to be with Rosalie, but I'll give him a ring as soon as I'm ready to leave.'

'It was good of you to stay with me, Stacy,' Liz whispered guiltily, 'and I'm sorry I've caused you so much trouble.'

'Don't be silly, my dear,' Stacy smiled warmly, but

her smile faltered a moment later. 'I'm sorry about what happened, though.'

'So am I,' Liz echoed from the deepest recesses of her heart. 'I should have listened to you and Pamela, but instead I went ahead and married a man who——'

'You said we wouldn't talk about him again,' Stacy interrupted firmly. 'What you have to concentrate on at the moment is getting better. Angus and I want you home as soon as possible.'

When Stacy left a few minutes later Liz lay awake and watched the sun rise. Grant's bronzed face leapt into her mind. 'I asked you to marry me at a time when I was at my lowest ebb, mentally and physically,' his voice tortured her.

'I hate you, Grant Battersby!' Liz whispered fiercely into the silent ward. 'Your thoughtless, callous behaviour took from me the only thing I still had left. I *hate* you! *I shall hate you for ever!*'

'She doesn't love you, you know. She never has, and she never will,' her own voice echoed back at her, then Grant's terse reply came relentlessly, like a tape being played over and over again, 'That's none of your business!'

'You fool! *You fool!*' Liz hissed into the silence. 'You love a beautiful face attached to a beautiful figure, and that's all Myra is. She's caught you in her trap, but she'll never love you as I do. *Never!*'

The tears came then, like a dam overflowing after a storm. She pushed her face into the pillow to try and stop them, but nothing helped, and great choking sobs tore at her aching throat until it felt raw. Tears were not going to help her at all, she knew that, but there was nothing she could do about it, and she wept like a child until she felt totally drained of emotion.

CHAPTER NINE

No matter how much she tried, Liz could not shake off her depression. She had forbidden the use of Grant's name, but that did not prevent her from thinking about him until the longing became intolerable. Six long, empty weeks had passed since Grant had hinted at a divorce, and still she had heard nothing from Joe Townsend. Every week, without fail, she received a cheque in the post from Grant, but every week she tore it up. She had accepted the Mini to please him, but she would not accept another cent from him.

Slowly, very slowly, her life regained a certain normality. During the day she managed to keep herself occupied with her writing, but it was the nights she hated most. That was the time when Grant haunted her most. Was he with Myra? Were they making love? *Please*, God, she did not want to think about it! Had she not been tortured enough?

Liz wanted to move out of Stacy's home into a place of her own, but Angus and Stacy would not hear of it. She could move out, they had said, when they had convinced themselves that she was well and truly on the road to recovery, but not before.

Another month passed, during which Liz sent off two manuscripts to her publisher in the hope of boosting her funds a little. She was beginning to feel more like her usual self, she could think and feel again, and one afternoon, while she was having tea with Stacy in the living-room, she broached the subject once more of finding herself a flat somewhere in town.

'You'll do nothing of the kind,' Stacy announced adamantly. 'You're staying here with us, and nowhere else.'

'Stacy, be sensible,' Liz groaned.

'Angus and I would love you to stay. We want you to think of this as your home.'

Liz swallowed down the lump in her throat. The tears came so easily these days, and she cried much too often for her own good. 'You're both absolute darlings, but I shall have to find a place of my own soon.'

'You could at least stay here until your divorce has been finalised.' Liz flinched inwardly, but Stacy obviously had no intention of stepping off this painful subject. 'Speaking of the divorce,' she said, 'shouldn't you have heard from a lawyer or something ages ago?'

Liz shrugged with elaborate carelessness. 'I have no idea how long these things take.'

'Well, I would have thought that after almost three months you would have heard something, even if it's some sort of notification that divorce proceedings are in progress.'

'I suppose I'll hear soon enough,' Liz brushed aside her remark distastefully.

'Liz . . . about Grant . . .'

'I don't want to discuss him,' Liz said sharply, her cup rattling in the saucer as a sign of her agitation when she placed it in the tray and rose to her feet.

'Do you hate him that much?'

Liz turned away and stared out into the sunlit garden without actually seeing anything. How *did* she feel about Grant? Did she hate him? She ought to despise him for the way he had treated her, and yet . . . she couldn't! *She missed him.* At night, when she went to bed, her arms felt empty, and she yearned for his warmth, his voice, his touch, and the hopeless longing would bring on the now familiar tears before she eventually went to sleep.

'I don't hate him,' Liz sighed, biting down hard on her quivering lip to steady it. 'I tried to, but I can't.'

'Then why won't you discuss him?'

'It hurts,' Liz croaked, swinging round to face her sister. 'Dammit, Stacy, it still hurts!'

All the agony and despair of her hopeless love was mirrored in her eyes, and in the trembling of her generous mouth. Stacy saw it, and she went at once to Liz's side.

'Oh, my dear, I wish there was something I could do for you,' she said, putting her arms around Liz.

'There's nothing anyone can do,' Liz whispered unsteadily, making a desperate attempt to pull herself together. 'I shall simply have to learn to live with it, that's all.'

How does one learn to live with heartache? Liz wondered afterwards. How does one learn to cope with a longing that cannot be assuaged? Would there ever come a time when a day would pass without thinking of Grant, or a night without dreaming of him? If only she could look forward to the future instead of looking back into the past, but everything that was of importance to her lay in the past. There was no future for her without Grant. There had never been anyone else; it had always been Grant, and no one else could ever take his place.

Two weeks later Stacy came into Liz's room to wake her from her afternoon nap with the news that she had a visitor. 'There's a Mr Townsend downstairs who wants to speak to you,' Stacy said.

'Townsend?' Liz sat up abruptly and brushed her hair out of her eyes with hands that shook. 'Joe Townsend?'

'That's the name he gave me, yes.'

'Tell him I don't want to see him,' Liz snapped, swinging her legs off the bed and feeling a little sick inside. 'If there's anything I have to sign, then he can leave the papers here, and I'll post them on to him.'

'He never mentioned anything about a divorce, Liz,' Stacy assured her. 'The only thing he said was that he had something of importance to discuss with you.'

'Such as?' Liz demanded cynically.

'He wouldn't say. He simply said to tell you it's a private matter, and of extreme urgency.'

Grant! There was something the matter with Grant! What else could it be? She was being ridiculous! Why would Joe come to her instead of Myra? Liz could not deny that she was curious, and more than just a little anxious.

'Tell him I'll be down in a minute,' she changed her mind abruptly, and when she was alone again she found that her insides were shaking almost uncontrollably.

News of Grant would be like manna from heaven, she admitted to herself when she brushed her hair and touched up her make-up, and her hands were still shaking a little when she smoothed down her skirt and checked her appearance in the mirror. She had lost weight, and the shadows beneath her eyes gave her a haunted, unfamiliar look, but in every other way she had matured. Her face was the face of a woman who had known passion and sorrow. The defiance of youth had departed to leave her totally unassuming; she expected nothing and dared not hope for anything.

She went downstairs, and hoped that she looked calmer than she felt at that moment. It felt like years instead of months ago that Joe had taken her to dinner to warn her of Myra's arrival in Johannesburg. So much had happened since then, and so many futile tears had been shed.

Joe came towards her when she entered the living-room, and her hands were gripped so tightly that her fingers ached.

'It's good to see you again,' he smiled down into her grave face, but the next instant his expression sobered. 'I was sorry to hear about the child you lost.'

'I suppose Stacy told you,' she remarked stiffly.

Joe hesitated briefly, then he released her hands and said sternly, 'Sit down, Liz. What I have to discuss with you concerns Grant.'

'I don't particularly want to discuss him,' Liz protested stubbornly when they sat facing each other in Stacy's homely living-room.

'All I ask is that you listen to what I have to say. If you don't want to discuss him, then that's fine with me, but at least listen to what I have to say,' Joe insisted with a note of urgency in his voice, and Liz found herself relenting against her will.

'Very well,' she sighed, 'I'm listening.'

'Grant is not himself. He's restless and he's drinking heavily,' Joe informed her without further dallying, and Liz did not quite succeed in hiding the shocked expression that flitted across her face. 'It started soon after you left, but since then it's become steadily worse. His work has always been the most important thing in his life, but he's hardly ever in his consulting-rooms these days, and he's seldom at the hospital.' Joe leaned towards her, his green eyes filled with concern. 'Grant has referred nearly all his patients to Alan Bishop, and I dread to think what might happen if he continues to behave in this manner.'

Liz stared fixedly at her hands in her lap, and tried desperately to remain detached from the information Joe was passing on to her. 'What do you expect me to do about it?'

'Talk to him, Liz. Try to reason with him, and make him see sense.'

Her face hardened, and her back went rigid. 'You're knocking on the wrong door, Joe. It's Myra you should be approaching, not me. She's the one who would have the most influence over him now.'

'Myra?' he frowned. 'What has Myra got to do with this?'

'You should know, Joe. Grant has surely approached you about seeking a divorce, hasn't he?'

'What divorce?' he demanded at once. 'What are you talking about?'

'Don't pretend with me, Joe,' Liz sighed irritably, getting to her feet and walking across to the window to stare out into the garden with its colourful display of spring flowers. There were signs of new life wherever she looked, but in her heart it would always be winter, she thought bitterly, and without turning she said: 'You know as well as I do that I left Grant so that he could be free to consider marriage to Myra.'

'My dear girl, I know nothing of the kind,' Joe denied emphatically, joining her in front of the window, and turning her to face him. 'Myra returned helter-skelter to Paris almost three months ago, and

Grant has certainly never mentioned anything to me about a divorce.'

Liz felt her heart lurch violently and, expelling the air slowly from her lungs, she said in a husky whisper, 'I don't think I understand.'

'That makes two of us,' Joe admitted, pushing his fingers through his thick mop of reddish-brown hair. 'Perhaps if I told you everything as I know it then we might both be able to make some sense out of this entire business.'

'Perhaps that would be a good idea,' she replied faintly, returning to her chair when it felt as though her legs would no longer take her weight.

'Acting on information I received from Alan Bishop, I went to see Grant a few evenings ago and found him . . .' Joe paused and smiled wryly as he seated himself opposite Liz, 'well, I won't say in what condition I found him, but with a lot of persuasion I finally managed to get him to talk. He was rather incoherent and distraught, but he mentioned something about sending you away, and that he blamed himself entirely for your miscarriage. I presumed, naturally, that you'd packed up and left him in a fit of temper after a serious disagreement, or something of the sort.'

Liz was pale and shaky. 'I never told him I was going to have a baby, so how did he know that I'd lost it?'

'I'm afraid I can't answer that,' Joe replied. 'What I *do* know is that guilt is practically driving Grant up the wall, and that's what's keeping him away from you.'

None of this quite made sense, and she cautiously adopted a sceptical attitude towards the information Joe had given her. 'What do you want me to do? Go and pat him on the head and tell him he need not feel guilty about me in future?'

'He loves you, Liz.'

His words fell like worthless seeds on dry, untilled soil, and she said in a brittle voice, 'He's never loved me, and he never will. He wanted me, that's all, and I was useful to him when he had needed someone to lean on, but it's Myra he loves. It's always been Myra.'

'Not any more, it isn't,' Joe persisted, and Liz did not have the energy nor the inclination to argue with him.

'Did Grant tell you where to find me?'

'No,' Joe shook his head. 'I asked him for your address, but he wouldn't give it to me, and told me to keep my nose out of his affairs. Later I recalled that he'd once mentioned the fact that your brother-in-law owned a service station here in Pietersburg, and I telephoned almost every one of them before Angus MacLeod finally gave me the answer I was looking for.' He leaned towards her again, his eyes intent upon her pale, pinched face. 'Liz, you've *got* to help Grant.'

'What makes you think he'll accept help from me?'

'He needs you, Liz, I'm almost sure of that, but he's too proud and too damn stubborn to admit it,' Joe growled. 'I gather he knows he's treated you badly, and he's convinced that you hate him for it as much as he hates himself.'

'I did hate him for a while, but I don't any more.' Liz stared down at the carpet and forcibly suppressed that flicker of hope that was struggling to the surface of her being. 'Why should you think that he loves me?'

'Why else would he be falling apart the way he is?'

Falling apart? Grant? Because of her? Impossible! 'It could be that he's pining for Myra.'

'I doubt it,' Joe snorted disparagingly. 'But even if

that was so, could you sit back and let him destroy himself in this way?'

Liz gestured helplessly with her hands. 'What do you suggest I should do?'

'Go and see him, that's all I ask.'

Liz recoiled from the idea. The house of mirrors was the last place on earth she would choose for a confrontation with Grant. There were too many unhappy memories there, and too many reminders that she would be stepping once again into Myra's domain.

'I have a better idea.' A crazy, stupid, mixed-up idea, she could have added. 'Do you think you could persuade him to come and spend a week or two on his farm?'

'I might be able to do that.' Joe eyed her thoughtfully. 'What have you got in mind?'

'I haven't quite decided yet, but if you let me know when to expect him, then I might just be there when he arrives.' If that was not asking for trouble, then she wondered what was.

'You don't want me to tell him this? You want to surprise him?' Joe asked, his familiar grin twisting his mouth and sparkling in his green eyes.

'The element of surprise occasionally has the desired effect,' she told him, his infectious grin succeeding in lifting the corners of her mouth. 'Did you come all this way merely to talk to me about Grant?'

Joe shrugged as if the distance did not matter. 'I couldn't very well discuss this delicate situation with you on the telephone, could I?'

'Are you staying the night?'

'I've booked myself into the hotel, and I'm leaving again first thing in the morning.'

'You must stay and have dinner with us this evening.'

'Well, I . . .'

'Please, Joe,' she begged. 'It would make me very happy if you accepted.'

Joe relented, and the evening passed quite pleasantly. Angus and Stacy accepted him as a friend of Liz's, and Joe's interest in cars gave Angus the opportunity to discuss the subject he enjoyed most.

Later that evening, when Liz walked out with Joe to his car, he said: 'I'll let you know as soon as I have definite information.'

'What if you're wrong? What if he doesn't want me?' she demanded anxiously.

'Then I hope you'll let me become one of your regular visitors,' Joe replied promptly, and Liz stared up at him in the darkness, not quite sure whether he was joking or not. His fingers brushed lightly against her cheek. 'Most men don't realise the value of what they've got until they come close to losing it. Hang on to that thought, Liz.'

He was driving away before she could think of a suitable reply, and once again that forlorn little hope reared its head, but she thrust it from her angrily.

Angus was still stretched out in his favourite chair and Stacy was clearing away the coffee cups when Liz entered the living-room. Something had niggled away at the back of Liz's mind all evening, and now she knew what it was.

'Stacy, did you tell Grant about my miscarriage?'

Stacy looked up sharply, but it was Angus who spoke. 'You'd better tell her, love,' he said. 'You can't hide the truth for ever.'

There was a spark of anger in Liz's eyes when she

faced her sister. 'You telephoned him after I'd asked you explicitly not to?'

'It was quite the opposite, I promise you,' Stacy contradicted quietly. 'Grant rang here the morning after you'd lost the—the baby. I was so choked up about everything that I'm afraid I let him have it.'

Liz felt a coldness shifting up into her cheeks. 'You told him everything?'

'Everything,' Stacy nodded, her cheeks stained with guilt.

'What did he say?'

'Nothing,' Stacy spread out her hands expressively. 'He was quiet for such a long time that I thought he'd passed out, or something, then he asked if he could come and see you. I told him no, he'd done enough harm, and that you'd been quite adamant about never wanting to see him again.'

Liz sat down on the arm of the chair behind her and stared down at her hands for a moment before she looked up curiously and asked, 'Did he say anything about Myra?'

Stacy shook her head. 'He never mentioned her. Why?'

'I believe Myra returned to Paris soon after I left Grant.'

'He never said a word,' Stacy assured her. 'Do you think——'

'I don't think anything,' Liz interrupted hastily. 'Not yet, anyway.'

She would not dare to hope too much at this stage while everything was still so bewildering. Myra had been so determined to get Grant, but she had walked out on him again the moment he was hers for the taking. What am I supposed to make of that? Liz wondered confusedly.

'You haven't told Liz everything,' Angus' voice interrupted her turbulent thoughts, and Liz glanced enquiringly at Stacy.

'Grant telephoned again about a month ago. He asked if I thought you'd see him, and I told him I didn't think so.' Stacy looked distressed and vaguely guilty. 'What else could I tell him, Liz? You refused to discuss him at the time, and you'd forbidden the mention of his name.'

'I'm not accusing you, Stacy,' Liz said calmly. 'You did exactly what I'd asked you to do.'

'The reason I didn't tell you about it is because I was afraid it would upset you,' Stacy explained, looking as though a great weight had rolled off her shoulders, then she eyed Liz curiously. 'What did Mr Townsend have to discuss with you?'

It would be no use hiding the truth from them, since they would know sooner or later, Liz decided, and neither would it be fair to keep them in the dark, so she related, almost verbatim, her entire conversation with Joe Townsend that afternoon. It took her several minutes, but they listened to her without interrupting.

'I suppose you think me crazy,' she groaned eventually when they simply stared at her without commenting. 'God knows, I should let him rot in hell, but I—I can't. I'll never forgive myself if I turned my back on him when he needed help desperately.'

It was so quiet in the living-room when she stopped speaking that one could have heard a pin drop, then Stacy said incredulously, 'You still love him? After everything he's done to you, you still love him?'

'I'll always love that stubborn, selfish, sometimes arrogant man. Heaven only knows why I love him, but he's always been the only man for me,' Liz confessed in an anguished voice and, getting to her feet, she fled upstairs to her room.

What she had said was the unvarnished truth. She loved Grant, and she would always love him. That was the reason she was contemplating this mad, crazy, impossible scheme . . . but what if it worked? What if Joe had been right in thinking that Grant loved her after all?

'Forget it! He feels guilty, that's all,' her mind warned with harsh cynicism, but her heart was beating out a rhythm of new hope, and she sighed into the silent darkness of her room, 'Grant, oh, Grant, please don't let me down this time!'

A week passed with agonising slowness, and yet another was drawing to its close before Liz heard from Joe.

'You can expect Grant out at the farm some time late tomorrow afternoon,' he told her over the telephone. 'It was a bit tricky, but between Alan Bishop and myself we managed to convince him that the fresh country air was exactly what he needed.'

Nervous excitement quickened her pulse rate. 'You don't think he suspects that I might have something to do with it?'

'He has no idea that you're in any way involved with this,' Joe laughed conspiratorially. 'There's one problem, though. How are you going to get into the cottage, or do you plan on arriving there after Grant has settled in?'

'I think I would prefer to be there when he arrives,' Liz replied. 'And getting hold of a key is no problem at all. Sam Muller keeps a spare on the farm.'

'That's a relief,' Joe sighed. 'All I can say to you now is, "best of luck".'

'I think I'm going to need it,' Liz laughed nervously.

When she put the receiver down a few moments later her legs felt like jelly, and she leaned heavily against the wall for support.

'I gather Grant is coming,' Stacy remarked shrewdly as she came down the stairs into the hall.

'He'll be at High Ridges some time late tomorrow afternoon,' Liz confirmed, chewing nervously at her bottom lip.

'What if that fails?' Stacy voiced Liz's fears. 'What if you simply get a flea in your ear for your trouble?'

'Then I will at least have the satisfaction of knowing that I tried, in some way, to help him.'

'And what about yourself?' Stacy asked sharply. 'What will you get out of it except more heartache?'

Liz sank her teeth into her lip once more. 'I shall have to take that risk.'

For many reasons it *was* a risk, and Liz could not deny it, but it was a risk which she knew she had to take. Grant would not come to her, not after she had been so adamant about not seeing him or speaking to him, and knowing that he had not instigated divorce proceedings made her entertain the vague hope that there was a slight possibility of their marriage being saved. On the strength of that vague hope she would take the chance, and risk the consequences.

Liz slept very badly that night, and she was up long before sunrise to draw up a list of the items she would require. Now that her plan was reaching its climax she found herself caught between nervousness and fear. There were so many things which could go wrong, and they were all too frightening to contemplate.

She sat down to breakfast with Stacy and Angus, but she was barely conscious of what she ate.

'Can we expect you back this evening?' Stacy broke the strained silence around the table.

'That depends,' Liz tried to smile. 'I'm taking an overnight bag with me, and if he wants me to I'll stay, but if I'm not welcome then you may expect me back before dinner this evening.'

'If I were Grant, then I'd be too ashamed to face you,' said Stacy, putting Liz's thoughts into words.

'That's exactly how I imagine Grant must feel,' Liz replied thoughtfully. 'And if I'm right, then there's a possibility after all that everything might work out for the best.'

'Don't build your hopes too high, lass,' Angus intervened, his rugged face showing concern. 'We wouldn't want to see you hurt all over again.'

'I'm not hoping for very much at the moment,' Liz sighed, pushing her plate aside. 'All I want is to talk to him, and to know once and for all where I stand. If it's only guilt he feels, then I want to know, but if it's more than that . . .'

Her voice trailed off into silence. There was no need to put into words what she was hoping and praying for, and before sunset that evening she would know whether she had simply been clinging once again to futile hopes and dreams.

Liz left the house a few minutes later to buy the supplies she wanted to take with her. It did not take her more than half an hour to do her shopping, and then she was driving out to High Ridges for the first time in many months.

CHAPTER TEN

TALL trees shaded the High Ridges homestead from the blazing November sun, and Sam Muller came out on to the wide *stoop* when he heard Liz's Mini come up the drive towards the house. She parked her car in the shade and got out quickly when she saw him coming towards her. Stockily built, and with a wide-brimmed hat shading his rugged, creviced face from the piercing rays of the sun, Liz discovered that he was only slightly taller than herself, and she hoped for some inexplicable reason that he was not going to make matters difficult for her.

Pale, watery grey eyes observed her with a touch of insolence from beneath the brim of his felt hat when she asked for the key to the cottage, and she experienced an unpleasant, crawling sensation beneath her skin.

'Dr Battersby will be here some time this afternoon,' he stalled.

'I know,' she said, curbing her impatience.

'Is he expecting you?'

'No,' she confessed, 'and I'm hoping that if he does touch on here you won't tell him that I'm at the cottage.'

'I don't know whether I should give you the key.'

'Why not?' she demanded sharply, annoyance sparkling in her eyes.

He stalled again, flicking that insolent glance over her, then he smiled nastily and drawled, 'Well, everybody knows that you and Dr Battersby haven't been living together these past months, and——'

'You're a good manager, Sam,' she interrupted him with a cold anger, 'but it appears you have an ear for anything that remotely resembles a scandal, and you obviously have a loose tongue to go with it. Now give me that key, or do I have to smash a window to get into my husband's cottage?'

His watery eyes widened. 'Dr Battersby wouldn't like that.'

'He'll like it even less if I should tell him that you refused me the key,' she added with a threatening note in her voice.

He glared at her and growled, 'There's no need to get nasty, Mrs Battersby. I'll get the key.'

That was not a good start, Liz thought unhappily when she drove away a few minutes later with the key to the cottage safely in her handbag. She hoped the day would end on a more favourable note. *Please, God, I pray that it does!*

Liz parked her Mini a little distance from the cottage where it would be carefully hidden among the trees, and she walked the rest of the way with her parcels. She felt a quick stab of pain when she glimpsed the cottage through the trees. There were so many memories locked up in that small cottage that she found herself pausing for a moment, hesitant to go farther, but she squared her shoulders almost at once, and walked on. Sam Muller had at least seen to it that the garden had been kept neat, and that was one more point in his favour.

She unlocked the door and went inside. A layer of dust coated the furniture, but everything else was exactly as they had left it. It was a matter of months, but it seemed as if endless years had passed in between. They had been happy here in this tiny cottage and, if Grant was willing, they could be happy here again, but Liz was faced with too much uncertainty to contemplate the future just yet.

She switched on the refrigerator and stacked the perishable food into it. After that she lost track of time while she dusted, swept, and polished. She stopped for a sandwich and a cup of coffee somewhere after twelve, then she aired the rooms and put clean linen on the bed, and when she finally had the opportunity to look at the time again she discovered that it was almost three o'clock in the afternoon. She made herself a quick cup of tea, and started the dinner. There had been no time to think, she had been too busy, but suddenly her doubts and fears returned with a vengeance, and she felt tense and jumpy at the least little sound.

The afternoon sun slanted in through the kitchen window, a dove called to its mate in the tree outside, and somewhere in the distance Liz could hear the cattle lowing in the fields. There was a peaceful tranquility in the air, but there was nothing peaceful or tranquil about the way Liz felt as she moved about the kitchen preparing dinner while the clock relentlessly ticked away the minutes and the hours. Four ... five ... five-thirty! How much longer could she stand the torture of not knowing?

At last she heard a car approaching the cottage. It stopped, a door slammed, and heavy footsteps crunched up the path towards the door. A key was inserted in the lock, and Liz felt her insides shaking uncontrollably. *Grant was here!*

Her hands fluttered to her hair, and she realised, to her horror, that her nose must be shining. It was too late to do anything about it now, she told herself ruefully and, pulling herself together with an effort, she tried to concentrate on the salad she was making, but every nerve in her body vibrated alarmingly when she heard Grant approach the kitchen. He paused in the doorway, she felt his eyes on her, and only then did she turn.

Shock coursed through her when she looked at the man who stood there staring at her. He looked haggard and drawn, the steel-grey eyes sunk deep into their sockets, and a grimness about his mouth that made her want to weep. He stared at her as if he thought he were seeing a ghost, and the tension in the air seemed to climb higher with every second that passed before he put down his suitcase and took a few steps into the kitchen.

'What are you doing here?' he demanded, his voice so harsh that it scraped uncomfortably along her nerve ends.

Play it cool, she warned herself and, in a voice that belied the turmoil inside her, she said: 'I decided that the cottage needed an airing, and I planned on spending the night, that's all.'

'Am I expected to believe that you happen to be here quite by chance at the very time I was advised to indulge in a brief holiday?' he questioned her cynically, his eyes never leaving her face for a moment.

'I don't expect you to believe anything, but if you want me to leave, then you only have to say so.'

His eyes narrowed. 'I believe you really mean that.'

'I do mean it.' Her heart was beating so hard and fast that it almost choked her when he lessened the distance between them to tower over her. The kitchen was all at once not big enough for both of them, but she raised her head with a touch of the old defiance to meet the onslaught of his eyes. 'If my presence here displeases you, then I'll leave at once, and taking into consideration that there's only one bedroom in this cottage, I'll have to leave after dinner anyway.'

His mouth twitched. 'I could always sleep on the sofa in the lounge and, considering that we're still married, no one will turn a hair.'

Liz turned away from the mockery in his eyes and glanced at the clock. 'There's time for you to shower and change into something comfortable before dinner.'

She picked up a tomato and sliced into it, praying that Grant would not notice how her hands were shaking. She felt him behind her, felt his eyes burning directly into her back, and then he was walking away from her. She sighed inwardly with relief when she heard him walk towards the bedroom, then she closed her eyes for a moment and leaned against the cupboard in an attempt to steady herself.

Liz had never seen Grant looking so dreadful before. She could not ignore the signs of suffering that lined his handsome face, and neither could she shut her mind to his sallow complexion. Could she be the cause of it, or was it Myra?

She heard him in the shower while she turned the steak and prepared the mushroom sauce. Everything else was ready, and she set out two glasses before she opened the bottle of wine she had chilled. All that remained was to spread a colourful cloth over the table and lay out the silver.

When Grant walked into the kitchen a half hour later he was dressed in blue denims and a red checked shirt with the sleeves rolled up to above his elbows. He looked refreshed, but no less haggard, she decided, finding it increasingly difficult to keep her eyes off him.

'Would you like a glass of wine before dinner?' she asked as casually as she could make it.

'I wouldn't mind a stiff whisky, but wine will do, thanks,' said Grant, his eyes following her when she turned away to pour the wine, and her nostrils quivered with the familiar smell of his masculine cologne when she handed him his glass. Their fingers touched briefly, sending something similar to a current of electricity up the length of her arm, and she almost snatched her hand away before he had the glass firmly in his clasp. 'Did you plan on wining and dining here alone?' he questioned her in a derisive voice.

'If I'd been expecting someone then they would have been here by now,' she replied stiffly, her trembling fingers tightening about the stem of the glass she raised to her lips.

'Or they might have gone back the way they came when they saw my car outside.'

'That's possible.'

'Unless, of course, you were expecting me.'

'That's possible too.' He was getting much too close to the truth for comfort and, putting down her glass, Liz gestured towards the table. 'If you will sit down over there then we can have our dinner.'

Liz dished up quickly, and they sat down to a silent meal. She could not eat, she was too conscious of Grant sitting at the opposite end of the small table, and neither did he appear to have a ravenous appetite. They sampled everything and drank their wine, but most of the dinner, which she had taken such pains to prepare, remained on their plates. She would have been content to simply sit there staring at him, but she forced herself not to, and neither did she dare voice the questions which she longed to have answered.

When she got up from the table to wash the dishes he picked up a towel and helped her to dry them. It was like old times, working silently side by side, only this time the silence was strained and filled with conflicting emotions.

'How often have you been here these past months?' he asked when everything was neatly packed away and the kitchen tidied.

'This is the first time,' she said nervously. 'And you?'

'First time.' His mouth tightened. 'I didn't want to come before this.'

'Neither did I,' she confessed, and their eyes met and held.

'Too many memories.'

Liz swallowed convulsively. 'For me too.'

She caught a glimpse of something in his eyes, but it was gone before she could analyse it.

'You never cashed the cheques I sent you,' he accused.

'I tore them to pieces and threw them away.'

'Why?'

'I have my pride too, Grant,' she told him with calm dignity.

'I've sold the house and moved back into my flat,' he said after an awkward silence had prevailed and, putting a cigarette between his lips, he cupped his hand around the flame of his lighter.

'I see,' she murmured, her heart lifting.

'I'm thinking of buying something else; something which could be converted into a real home.'

'That's nice,' she remarked with false casualness

while everything within her rejoiced at the knowledge that the house of mirrors was no longer in his possession.

Grant was silent for a long time, but she was conscious once again of his eyes following her about while she made coffee and poured it into mugs. It was almost dark outside, and she switched on the light in the kitchen before she joined him at the table. She raised her mug to her lips and their eyes met across the table. There was something in those steel-grey depths that made her catch her breath, and her heart jolted wildly in her breast before it raced on at a frantic pace.

'I've made a mess of everything, haven't I?'

He spoke quietly and without his usual mockery, and her compassionate heart went out to him. 'Every storm leaves a little damage in its wake, but the damage is seldom irreparable.'

His eyes burned into hers, and his mouth twisted with something which resembled self-derision. 'Would you say there's anything left to salvage?'

'That depends entirely on you.'

Grant's hand moved towards hers across the checkered tablecloth, but instead of touching her, he pushed back his chair and rose to his feet with an angry exclamation on his lips. He stood staring out of the window at the inky blackness of night shifting across the veld, and his thumbs were hooked into the broad belt that hugged his denims to his lean hips.

'I forfeited the right to expect anything when I threw away a precious jewel for a paste diamond with a false glitter,' he said harshly without turning to face her, but she saw the muscles jutting out along the side of his jaw, and she knew that he was struggling with a fierce emotion that was finding an echo in her. 'I'd give anything now to possess again what I so callously discarded, but one can never go back in time to correct one's mistakes.'

'We *have* gone back in time,' she argued softly, but there was a note of urgency in her voice as she rose quickly to join him there beside the window. The longing to touch him was so intense at that moment that she had to clench her hands at her sides, and the flame of hope in her heart was being fanned into a blazing fire. 'We're here,' she heard herself say unsteadily. 'Just the two of us ... and we could start again, if that's what you want.'

'It's not what I want, Liz.' He swung round to face her, and his face bore such a tortured expression that she had to restrain herself with the greatest difficulty from flinging her arms about his neck and comforting him. 'For the first time in my selfish life I find myself considering someone else's needs before my own, and that's the only reason why I stopped short of coming up here to Pietersburg and demanding that you see me when I knew that you had no wish to do so.'

A joyous warmth invaded her heart and spilled over until it seemed to fill her entire body. Grant was, in his own peculiar way, saying that he cared, but that invisible barrier was still there between them.

'Tell me about Myra,' she came right to the core of the problem, and Grant flinched as if she had struck him.

'I think I must have been mad, but for six years she had an almost physical hold on me which I couldn't break. After the accident I felt bitter towards her and the whole human race, then you came along and life became bearable once more. I thought I'd got over Myra, but when I saw her in that restaurant I knew

I'd imagined it. I was hooked again, and there appeared to be nothing I could do about it, but that only lasted until Myra came to see me the day after you'd gone. I looked at her then and discovered to my dismay that I felt absolutely nothing for her. Heaven help me, Liz!' he groaned, his voice hoarse and almost unrecognisable. 'It was like waking up from one nightmare and plunging straight into another, and it was sheer *hell*! All I could see was a beautiful body, and quite suddenly I was no longer blind to the rest of her. She possessed none of the qualities I could admire in a woman, and that was when I was hit with the stunning realisation of what I'd done. I wanted *you*; I wanted your warmth, and your sweet, generous soul, and . . . I'd sent you away in the most brutally callous manner.'

'You could have come after me.'

'Not after the telephone conversation I had with Stacy.' His eyes were feverishly bright as they burned down into hers. 'I'll never forgive myself for being the cause of your miscarriage, and in a few choice words Stacy told me exactly what she thought of me.' He looked white and shaken, and totally unlike himself. 'She told me that you never wanted to see me again— that you'd forbidden the use of my name.'

'I was hurt, and I imagined that I hated you, but . . .' She paused, fighting against the lump in her throat and the painful memories. 'It didn't last very long,' she finally added in a choked voice.

'I spoke to Stacy again a month ago, and she told me that you still refused to have anything to do with me,' he went on as if she had not spoken, and his hand shook when he raked his fingers through his dark hair with the silver wings against his temples. 'I went a little mad after that, I think.'

'Grant . . .' She could not stand his tortured expression a moment longer and, taking his face between her hands, she whispered huskily, 'I've never stopped loving you.'

His fingers gripped her wrists lightly, and his mouth was like fire against her left, then her right palm and, to her horror, she saw there were tears in his eyes.

'Can you ever forgive me?' he asked softly.

'I've forgiven you long ago.'

'I never dared hope for more than that.'

She could not bear to see him so humble. It brought hot tears to her eyes and an aching lump to her throat. 'If you want me, Grant, all you have to do is say so.'

'I want you,' he groaned, and then she was in his arms, her softness yielding against the hard length of him as they kissed and kissed again with a hunger which would not be easily assuaged. They had been apart too long, and their need of each other had become too intense to be satisfied with kisses and wild caresses, and Liz almost cried out in protest when Grant dragged his lips from hers to bury his face against the smooth hollow of her throat. 'I never knew how much I wanted you until you were no longer there, and then it was too late,' he said thickly, his arms tightening about her as if he were afraid she would try to get away from him. 'It was like looking in those mirrors and discovering with a shock that you'd gone, your image was no longer there beside me like a breath of fresh air in that revolting house. That was when I took a long, harsh look at myself, and what I saw made me feel physically ill. I was more than just disgusted with myself, I was——'

'Hush!' she interrupted him in a voice that shook

with emotion. 'Don't say anything more.'

His mouth shifted over hers with a hungry yet tender passion that stirred her to the very depths of her soul, and she responded with all the love that was there in her heart for him. His hands slid over her hips, drawing her closer into the hard curve of his body, and making her aware of his need. Time stood still, there was no past or present, and she locked her arms about his strong neck with the knowledge that the long, eternal night of unhappiness was at last at an end. The future was like the dawning of a new day with the promise of better things to come.

'Shall we start again?' she asked when they both paused a moment to draw breath.

'I can't think of anything I want more than that,' he smiled, framing her face in his hands, and there was a light in his eyes that made her hold her breath. She wanted to capture that look, and hold it to her heart for ever. 'I love you, Liz. I love you better than life itself, and that's something I never thought I would ever say to a woman,' he whispered against her lips, and it was to her the sweetest music she had ever heard.

Those long-awaited words soothed away the hurt and the months of suffering as nothing else could have done, and her expression was tremulous with an inner radiance. 'I thought I'd never hear you say that you loved me.'

'I swear I'll spend the rest of my life proving to you just how much I love you,' he said thickly, his hands moulding her to him with a new urgency. 'I need you, Liz. I can't exist without you there to bully me, or scold me, and I know now that the day simply doesn't begin for me unless I hear your voice and know you're close enough to touch.'

'Oh, Grant,' she whispered, tears of happiness hovering on her lashes. 'Forgive me for crying, but I'm so happy.'

Later that night, when they lay in each others arms in the darkened bedroom, Grant said: 'When Joe and Alan first suggested this short holiday I rejected the idea, but it finally began to appeal to me. I thought that, if fate was kind, I would see you somehow and work things out from there.'

'Instead you found me here the moment you arrived, and you certainly didn't look very pleased about it,' she accused teasingly.

'I was stunned, and I was scared out of my wits that I might do or say something that would make you walk out on me.' His hand tightened on her hip. 'Whose idea was it, anyway?'

'Mine,' she confessed, turning her face into his shoulder. 'Joe came to see me. He was concerned about you, and when he told me that you hadn't filed for a divorce, I—I hoped there was just a tiny chance that you might care enough to resume our marriage.'

'I was a fool, a crass idiot,' he growled, 'and I'm amazed that you can forgive me when I——'

She turned his face towards hers and silenced him with a kiss. 'I love you, Grant. I always have, and I always will. That's all there is to it.'

She kissed him again, but when she would have drawn away his hand went up to the nape of her neck, and he held her there. Their kiss deepened, became passionate and demanding, and she yielded to the touch of his hands. The intimacy of his caresses aroused her and awakened again that achingly familiar need, and once again that night Liz held nothing back, giving as much as she was receiving until she was plunged into that mystical world where only Grant could take her. She was alive again, she was his woman, and he wanted her.

Liz stood on the terrace of their home and watched the setting sun cast lengthy shadows across the spacious garden which covered more than an acre. Grant had bought this lovely old house on the outskirts of Johannesburg shortly after their return to the city, they had moved in a month later, and now, after another three months of planning and hard work, they had turned it into a dream of a home in which they could entertain their friends, or simply relax. Liz was happier than she had ever been, but her eyes were clouded and troubled on that afternoon when she turned from the peaceful scene outside and walked into the house. Grant had warned her that he would be home late that evening. On such evenings he usually had a quick meal at the hospital, so she fixed herself a snack and tried to read for a while, but she found that her concentration was low.

She wished that Grant would come home, but when the hands of the clock shifted towards nine o'clock she set her book aside and went upstairs. She was in the bath when she finally heard Grant's Jaguar come up the drive, and she relaxed completely for the first time since that afternoon.

A few minutes later she heard him entering their bedroom, and his footsteps sounded heavy and tired. When she came out of the bathroom five minutes later she found him sprawled on the bed. He had removed his jacket and tie, his shirt was unbuttoned to the waist, and he had kicked off his shoes.

'You look as though you've had a rough day,' she said, fastening the belt of her silk robe about her waist as she approached the bed and sat down beside him.

'One of the worst,' he grimaced, his hand slipping beneath the golden veil of her hair to pull her head down until their lips met in a lingering kiss. 'How was your day?' he asked when she was allowed to breathe freely again.

'So-so,' she shrugged casually, her lashes veiling a secretive light which had crept into her eyes. 'I messed about in the garden for a while, then I went out shopping, and I paid a visit to that nice old doctor on the third floor of the medical centre.'

'Liz?' His eyes probed hers questioningly, then his arm was about her waist and she was pulled across him so that she ended up lying beside him on the bed. He leaned over her, his tiredness apparently forgotten, and there was an incredulous light in his eyes. 'You're pregnant?'

'For a medical man you've been rather obtuse, haven't you?' she teased, raising a hand to trace the outline of his strong mouth, and he caught her hand in his to nibble sensually at the tip of her finger.

'I've been too busy enjoying my wife to think of anything else.'

'How does the thought of becoming a father appeal to you?'

'It appeals to me very much.'

'Grant . . .' There was something so erotic about the fiery caress of his tongue against the palm of her hand that she knew she had to say what was on her mind before it was too late. 'I bumped into Alan Bishop when I left the medical centre this afternoon, and he told me that—that Myra was back in Johannesburg for a while.'

'I know,' said Grant, taking her hand and pressing it against his warm, hair-roughened chest where she could feel the hard, even beat of his heart beneath her fingers. 'I saw her briefly this afternoon.'

'And?' she prompted, holding her breath.

'And nothing,' he smiled down at her in that old, twisted manner. 'She tried her level best to convince me that what we had together once was something special, and that there was no reason why we couldn't recapture it, but I'm afraid it didn't work this time. She's a very beautiful woman, but I have everything I could ever want right here in my arms, and you're more precious to me than anything or anyone else in this world.' He caught a teardrop on the tip of his finger before it rolled very far down her cheek. 'Why are you crying?'

'I'm just so terribly happy, that's all,' she sighed tremulously.

'Silly girl,' he mocked her gently. 'Do you trust me now, and believe that I love you?'

'I *know* you love me, and I do trust you, but I—I couldn't help being a little afraid.'

Grant's fingers tugged at her belt, then his hand was beneath her robe, sliding across her flat stomach and upwards to cup the swell of her breast.

'You won't be afraid again, will you?' he asked against her mouth.

'I'll never be afraid again of losing you, my darling,' she whispered unsteadily, her lips parting beneath his, and her pulse rate quickening to match his.

She need never fear Myra again, Liz knew that now. She had not doubted Grant, but that niggling fear had always been there that Myra might still have some sort of hold over him. The chains of the past had at last been severed, and warm and secure within her was the product of her love for Grant, and the love which she no longer doubted he had for her.

Harlequin® Plus
A WORD ABOUT THE AUTHOR

Yvonne Whittal's childhood was spent in Port Elizabeth, on the southern tip of Africa. She recalls dreaming of the day she would be able to travel to unknown countries.

At a very early age she began scribbling stories. Her ambition to be a writer resurfaced after her marriage and the birth of three daughters. She enrolled in a writing course, began submitting short stories to publishers and, with each rejection letter, became all the more determined.

Turning to the task of writing a full-length book, Yvonne was encouraged by a young woman with whom she was working—an avid reader of romance fiction and a helpful critic.

For Yvonne Whittal, there is no greater satisfaction than writing. "The characters become part of my life," she says, "and when I come to the end of each novel, realizing that I now have to part with my manuscript, it is like saying farewell to dear and trusted friends."

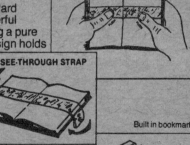

Harlequin Romances

The books that let you escape
into the wonderful world of romance!
Trips to exotic places...interesting
plots...meeting memorable people...
the excitement of love....These are
integral parts of Harlequin Romances –
the heartwarming novels read by
women everywhere.

Many early issues are now available.
Choose from this great selection!

Choose from this list of Harlequin Romance editions.*

Some of these book were originally published under different titles.